The Healer From Qumran:

A Spiritual Journey of Divination, Healing, and Awakening in Biblical Time

BY ADIYA SHAPIRA

Producer & International Distributor
eBookPro Publishing
www.ebook-pro.com

The Healer from Qumran
Adiya Shapira

Copyright © 2023 Adiya Shapira

All rights reserved; no parts of this book may be reproduced or transmitted in any form or by any means, electronic or mechanical, including photocopying, recording, taping, or by any information retrieval system, without the permission, in writing, of the author.

Translation: Sharon Singer
Editing: Mathew Berman

Contact: adiyashapira1@gmail.com

ISBN 9798870664637

Asaf

Introduction

In the dead of the night, I sneaked out to the field behind my house barefoot, wearing nothing but a tunic. I began to dig a pit to bury the scrolls of wisdom I had spent a year writing. The scent of damp soil of early winter days found its way to my nose as I rushed to dig as deep as I could to plant the clay pot containing my enshrouded scrolls.

I learned to write scrolls of wisdom several years earlier before I left the Essenes cult from my teacher Asa who shared with me the secrets of spiritual healing, as I was a strong candidate to succeed him as the leader of the Essene Unity Congregation. I wanted to hide the scrolls along with my fears and to subdue the pain and fear of death that enveloped me. Perhaps I would grant my scrolls a temporary death? Will I return to my scrolls and revive them in the future? And maybe when I return to exhume them, they will then be sought after as a hidden treasure. My scrolls contain the words of my teacher, Jesus, son of Joseph, as I interpreted them during our travels across the land of Israel this past year. I sat close to him, at his feet, and heeded his words with great thirst.

I wanted to witness him perform the wonders he told, to see the great teacher live as he preached. Alas, it would be better if the scrolls lay in the ground. I am endangering my life and the lives of my entire family with my forbidden writing. In the corner of my eyes, I envisioned him once again, the white owl with golden eyes, appearing in my life to support me in moments of exaltation, crisis, or fear. The owl, who accompanies and guides me, sat in the dark on the branch of an oak tree and stared at me, asking me to stop refusing to meet the "shadow" in me and to heal the wound in my soul, to see what is in the darkness in me and grow out of acceptance and love. The owl is waiting for me to understand that the world and my soul now want to move forward intertwined. The pain in me will now be transformed into light! The owl whispers to me, "You can listen to your true inner self and all its faces and create a new and optimal reality for you in the present."

Indeed, I am in a safe place again. I returned to live in the village where I was born, but rumors are circulating throughout the Land of Israel. A death sentence awaits Jesus, who was proclaimed enemy of the Jewish faith by the priests and leaders. The Romans who seek to kill him pose a great threat as well… Oh, so much fear and dread. And despite the dangers lurking in his life, Jesus courageously spreads his gospel of unity throughout the land, and I am his messenger.

I recall what Jesus son of Joseph told me, "Asaf, God is in you, be the light, spread it your way from within you." I labored for hours writing my scrolls, with enthusiasm, passion, and fear that Jesus' adversaries might catch me and put me to death. I carry along with me the fear of death also because I had witnessed a sad death last year, which led me to leave the Essenes after suffering a deep mental crisis. The council members of the Essenes tried Nimrod, my beloved cousin and best friend, and sentenced him to death by stoning. I watched the execution with other sect members, until he perished.

About a year has passed since I left the Essenes in Qumran. Since then, I married my beloved Miriam, whom I had met in the Essene sect, and we are now the parents of a newborn girl we have named Sara. But where did this nightmare begin? How did I find myself, Asaf the son of David, a simple farmer from a village at the foot of Mt. Tabor, involved in such bloodshed? Will Asa, my Essene teacher resume my spiritual training to ascension even though I left the cult? Will we be able to realize our common destiny, as he promised would happen on the day that I marry Miriam?

Chapter 1

I recall how my cousin Nimrod approached me several years ago one Spring afternoon asking me to join him and the Essenes. I had just finished sowing my father's field, and I was taking a much-needed rest under the olive trees. I tranquilly stared at the grooves left by my father, my cousins and their father who upturned the soil with the help of a plow and two donkeys.

I was my mother Hannah's only child, as she could not bear any more, and my cousin Nimrod was like a brother to me. My father and mother raised me as an only child wrapped in much love. I did not feel I missed having siblings, because I had Nimrod. My mother and I would have many heart-to-heart conversations and our souls were deeply intertwined. I would always try to offer comfort as she could not have any more children despite her wish for a large family. She stopped trying to get pregnant once she reached a certain age and that bothered her tremendously.

My father Abner taught me his farming crafts in my early childhood days. We would leave the house together at dawn and when we returned from the fields at noon, my mother would wait for us with a hot meal. Each day after lunch, my father and I would spend time at his workshop creating wooden furniture such as shelves, tables, and chairs, which we would sell in the village and at the local market. I inherited my father's expert hands and learned the secrets of healing ailments with herbs from my mother, who together with my father's sister Elisheva would treat family members and other villagers.

Nimrod and I spent many hours together. We were practically inseparable. We lived in the same village and would run around the meadows, playing and laughing together. Our extended family gathered frequently for large feasts and holiday celebrations. Nimrod's oldest sister was Shoshana, followed by two brothers older than him. He was the youngest of four. His father Jacob was a farmer who was deeply attached to his older sons Reuben and Dan, with whom he worked closely in the fields. Shoshana was extremely close with her mother, whom she helped with the housework and caring for the grandchildren.

Nimrod felt like deadwood and had much difficulty finding his place in his large family.

He grew up alone feeling somewhat rejected, partly because of the age gap between him and his siblings, which made communication and understanding quite difficult. His parents were old and too tired to raise him at that point in their lives, which made him grudgingly independent. I remember Nimrod as a sensitive boy, walking in the yard unkempt, barefoot, and his nose constantly runny. He would regularly hear the adults urging and rushing him to do his chores. He was told to sweep the yard and chop firewood. When he was a little bit older, he was tasked with feeding the animals that lived in the large court, donkeys, chickens, horses, sheep, and a cow.

When he turned thirteen, he started herding the family's livestock in the pastures surrounding the village where he would spend hours on his own. When he would return home, his father and brother would usually greet him with a scolding and lashes as a glutton for punishment for his impatient father's rage.

His father would often critique his work, for example when he lost a sheep that broke away from the herd, or if he was late to return home and herd the sheep into the pen before sunset. I do not recall him ever receiving words of encouragement or praise for anything from his father or brother. Positive reinforcements would come only from his mother and sister. Nimrod made his way through life with great difficulty, lacking self-esteem, without appreciation from those around him, no love, and deep anguish in his heart. He was angry with his mother and sister and blamed them for spoiling and praising him to compensate for his father who turned his back on him. His family dynamic was a lot for him to bear. Nimrod loved to walk alone in the fields of the village, humming tunes he made up and playing with a wooden flute he crafted with his own hands. The tunes provided comfort. He made a flute for me as well and taught me to play it despite my many hesitations. Nimrod supported and egged me on until I managed to confidently play an entire tune from start to finish.

Whenever I had time to spare, I would join him for long walks. We were happy together, but there were days when I came to pick him up and found him sobbing his eyes out, after being scolded by his father. Nimrod cried and cursed his father with his repeated "Damn you, Son of Belial," I would walk over to give him a hug without saying a word and usher him to the clearing, where he would calm down. And after we would spark fire and light, we then played the flutes together. We each had a role. Nimrod composed melodies for the songs, and I wrote the lyrics. He liked my words and always asked me to match new lines to his tunes. We created "songs of longing," which expressed love and yearning for another life, an illuminating life of happiness, a life we imagined was waiting for us and for which we were ready. We felt our lives were ahead of us, hopeful and happy in our joint creation, especially when we sang one particular song, the words of which I wrote on a tree, and which we sang every day.

> In the dark of night, the light of your heart like a star, twinkles
> And a moon illuminates your pinnacle.
> I shall look through the flowers of your spirit-splashed lavender,
> The tree of love filled with whisper.
> Whispers of the King, the Tree of Life,
> From whose zenith I shall pluck stars,
> Climb atop his bark and view as a spectator,
> His branches and leaves I shall carry as a scepter.
> As my own body and soul is my friend, the timber,
> On his beloved treow I shall linger.

The cold and storm will not make us fear.
To the place we go and from which we run,
We will rise up and ascend to the One.

In the clearing, when we talked about his difficulties, Nimrod comforted my loneliness and allowed me to offer him care and encouragement. He was the brother I never had. I wanted to protect and save him from his hurt. That is the reason he called me "Asaf the doctor" when he wanted to tease me. "Asaf the doctor." Thus, little by little, the dream of becoming the "village healer" was woven into my thoughts. I loved watching my mother concoct ointments from plants and pain-relieving oils, and I wanted to learn herbal medicine. However, Nimrod wanted to leave the village and wander to faraway places, striving to broaden his horizons and succeed in all his pursuits of selling sheep, cows, and donkeys. Growing up, I watched Nimrod raise himself. He denied every fear and the agony hidden inside as he set off to conquer the world. In his youth he clashed wildly with others, cursed, and beat them, contested against all odds even with those older than him. He also often quarreled with his brother and father, and with anyone who tried to prevent him from advancing or achieving the goal that his soul longed to seize and achieve. I saw the cruelty hidden in his soul as a small seed that was often violent. Cruelty he learned from his father's attitude towards him, which was made obvious to me and the whole family.

Chapter 2

I was twenty-five when Nimrod asked me to join him in the desert on the shores of the Dead Sea, to a wonderful and mysterious place where the Essene community resided. They were also known as the Unity Congregation and its members practiced deep spiritual Torah studies and lived a holy life. Nimrod had grown into a tall, gracious, and charismatic man who constantly wore a mischievous look on his face while his wise, dark eyes shined. That and the hardships of his childhood shaped his tough exterior, but he was not able to fool me. Even when he showed unwavering self-confidence, I knew that he was fragile and needed me as his support, just like when we were kids. I looked with admiration at my handsome and tanned friend who spent much of his time in the sun working in the meadow, and at his black mane of hair that was so different from my red hair. Nimrod was only one year older than me, and had an opinionated, authoritative, principled personality. He said that if I joined him with the Essenes, it would be an opportunity for me to realize my abilities and fulfil my destiny as a healer. "And to the place we go and from which we run, we will rise up and ascend to the One..." he sang the words of the tree song that became our private anthem as children. The truth is that I went with Nimrod to the Essenes, also because I wanted to protect him from himself. He was right about finding a vocation, but I did not think that the path to becoming a healer would be filled with so many twists and turns.

"Stop wasting your time on ordinary mundane work." he scolded. "Come with me to a place full of life, where you can finally become the healer that you have aways dreamed of being.

"I have already visited the Essenes and talked about it with distant relatives of ours, a brother and a sister, who were orphaned several years ago," said Nimrod. "They were accepted into the cult and living in the settlement, waiting for us to join them. Two months ago, at my mother's request, I went to check on their wellbeing. I knew after my visit there, that the place is right for me and for you."

The idea captivated me. I wanted to meet more relatives, expand my horizons, alleviate my loneliness as an only child. I gazed into Nimrod's playful smile and agreed. Even as a child, I would follow Nimrod's bold suggestions. I was fascinated by him, and at the same time, I worried about him and watched over him lest he get into trouble. I followed his lead to new adventures, but with a sense of tense restlessness gripping me. I remember how when we were children, he took me one fine day to the edge of the forest near our village, to see a hidden beehive. He thought of a way in which we could scare them away and take their honeycomb. He took a wooden branch he found on the ground, lit it from the small bonfire he had sparked and threw it burning into the hole of the ancient oak trunk that housed the hive.

We then saw a swarm of sleepy bees rush out of the hive flying panicky in every direction. Oh, it was the most terrifying sight indeed. Luckily, I was spared from any stings, because I started running quickly back to the village, leaving Nimrod behind, stung, cursing, and shouting "Damn bees" loudly. Nimrod, who was close to the beehive, stayed to take the honeycomb no matter what, and his entire body was throbbing with beestings. He later spent many days lying in his bed. His mother Elisheva cared for him and dressed his wounds with the special healing ointment known to the women in our family. She applied the ointment several times each day until he recovered from the beestings. When I came to visit, I felt guilt and shame for running away instead of helping him. Choking on my own tears, I told him I was sorry and that I was deeply concerned.

Nimrod smiled and tried to make me feel better. "Asi," he said, amused, in an attempt to ease my guilt, "I must have tried to take the bees' fruit of labor prematurely, so she gave me her sting and none of her honey." He mockingly uttered the words slowly, crinkling his swollen face as he drew out the syllables. "Am I to ask the forgiveness of the 'queen bee' for breaking into her home, destroying her world?" he said and chuckled. He continued talking and playing with words, rhyming. Every now and then, he laughed with a face contorted in pain, and I started rolling with uncontrollable laughter. The sting wounds hurt him when he moved his body and face while he laughed, which made us both laugh even harder. So was Nimrod. Actions before thoughts and happy to find joy in everything and anything, and so understanding of me. Despite my fears and past experiences on my adventures with Nimrod, I decided to go with him now toward the new dream of a meaningful life with the Essenes. To fulfil our destiny. I would become a healer, bearing peace wherever I would go. This was my chance to leave the village and broaden my world. I was so happy that Nimrod presented me with the opportunity to break out of life as a farmer and carpenter in our tiny village on Mt. Tabor. I was excited to leave the village I had spent my entire life along with my beloved cousin to a mysterious place near the Dead Sea in our country's southern region.

Nimrod said, "Grab a small knapsack for the journey, with a little food and some water. I heard that the Essenes would give us modest clothes and everything we need. These people lead very modest lives." Days later, I said goodbye to my mother and father once I shared the news that Nimrod and I were moving to the south of Israel to join the Essenes. I felt that I had reached maturity, that is, the right age to leave my parents' house and go off on my own independent path. My parents encouraged me to go the way I chose and where I wanted. It took us about a week to hike on the road from Mount Tabor in the north to the Dead Sea in the Judean Desert. We felt like friends uniting for an adventure; two young people leaving the known and familiar travelling toward the unknown. On our journey, we entered small villages, where we ate our bread, and filled our waterskins with fresh water. At night, we stopped in towns along the way, to visit friends and relatives. We stayed with them, and they accommodated us and hosted us generously, as commanded by the hospitality mitzvas customary of our land. Nimrod often talked and voiced his spiritual ideas in the ears of our hosts. Even if they did not understand anything of his speeches, he continued to ramble on with idealistic descriptions of his belief in light and purity. He shared with all of us his dream of realizing a spiritual study and living in a spiritual community, dedicated to a spiritual life and the love of God out of shared values of purity.

When he spoke, I listened to him attentively and was filled with hope and happiness thanks to his compelling enthusiasm. I also longed to reach the desert and meet the Essene community. We arrived at the settlement of Qumran which was located in the Judean desert west of the Dead Sea. The sun began to set as we approached the Dead Sea, and an amazingly beautiful scenery was revealed before us. We watched the mountain cliff stretching down, the rocks of a wild landscape, and the Dead Sea rift painted in deep blue. On our way, we saw streams flowing between the rocks and mysterious caves, hidden in stone, and scattered along the cliff. The silence was abysmal, both full of life and lifeless, an eternal silence of death and rebirth. Not a single person was there when we finally got to Qumran's Essene community. "Where are all the people?," I asked at the entrance to the village. In the distance, we saw a young woman walking hastily toward us. She was a good looking, short and energetic young woman of about twenty, wrapped in white scarves, wearing a simple white dress. Her long golden hair draped on her shoulders. "Hello Nimrod and Asaf," she said happily when she saw my cousin Nimrod, whom she knew. A small laugh graced her beautiful blue eyes as she spoke. "Thank God you arrived safely," she said and bowed benevolently to Nimrod and added in a pleasant and soft voice, "I have been waiting all day to greet you, to meet you and Asaf... My name is Miriam, and Nimrod told me that you are the son of Abner, a cousin of my late mother. I have come to take you to where you will be living. The members of our congregation are at evening prayers and Torah studies, so you will see them tomorrow."

"Follow me," she said with confidence and pride, as a guide on duty. She began to walk lightly towards a cave on the side of the mountain, which was allocated to us for accommodation. My heart skipped a beat when I stood by Miriam's side. Her physical beauty moved me, and the idea of living in a cave, which like a womb protects before a new birth, fascinated me. I felt at ease in the village, and it even seemed to me that I had known Miriam, my father's relative, forever. The images of Qumran began to unfold as we followed Miriam. We passed by a large complex of buildings which, as Miriam pointed out, served the members of the entire community in their cooperative lives. Miriam expounded, "Around the complex of these buildings there are about thirty caves, in which some of us live, and in addition to that there are members who live in tents or huts, all suited to their needs." She went on to explain that "there are sixteen bodies of water in Qumran, of which about ten are large *mikvehs* and purification baths, where members of the sect are baptized in water. The buildings are used for communal activities such as prayer, learning and for crafting during the five-hour workday. There is also one common dining hall for everyone, which includes a pantry and a kitchen. "We currently have about one hundred and fifty men living in the community, and a few women who provide us with services. Here they find refuge from their previous lives. We live as a community by strict laws of purity and impurity. We grow our own food and wear white clothes. Life here is remarkably simple.

"Every person who comes to Qumran goes through processes of purification and transformation, accompanied by at least one teacher, who prepares them for their spiritual ascension and their destiny. For example, Asa, whom you will surely meet soon, is my teacher and he might be yours too. Mutual assistance and charity are particularly important to our community. We have an elected council comprised of twelve members who serve as our leadership." She ended her words by saying, "See you tomorrow, and thank God that you arrived safely." She parted with us at the entrance to the cave and went about her business.

The cave we moved to was magical and mystically silent. We noticed thick white handmade wax candles, scattered in the corners of the cave, spreading sweet honey aromas. The candles illuminated the interior of the cave with a gentle light, and the movement of their flames was reflected in the shadows that danced on its walls. Mats made from palm branches were placed on the ground and on top of them blankets woven from sheep's wool, the handiwork of the locals. We lay down exhausted from our long journey on foot, and the hard ground, to which we were not accustomed, absorbed our bodies. Nimrod immediately fell asleep, and his breathing became heavy yet steady, while I remained awake. I could not quite calm down from the experiences of the last few days and the excitement from meeting with Miriam. Her beautiful figure rose again in my imagination, and I felt enchanted by her. One last and illogical thought popped into my mind and disrupted my rest, before I fell asleep for the rest of the night. It was evoked by the scent of honey that dispersed in the cave. The scent reminded me of the story of the honeycomb we coveted from the bees when we were kids. I asked myself, will Nimrod want to reach for the honeycomb again? Will something he does result in another sting?

Chapter 3

We went to bed early as the sun set yesterday, but the amassed fatigue from the past week on the road led us to wake up only at noon. We awoke to the sound of men's voices calling their friends to join them for a dip in the mikvah before the communal lunch in the dining hall. Nimrod woke up and slowly stretched before he jumped up from his bed with great enthusiasm. He wore cotton clothes according to the local custom - white pants and a long white shirt as a dress, which the cult members left for us at the edge of the cave. The clothes he wore were one or two sizes too big and sagged a little on his body. He started waving the oversized sleeves in the air, making us both laugh. He then folded the sleeves of the dress up to his elbows with much effort, and I did the same when I put on the garment that was waiting for me. "There must be giants living here going by the size of the clothes they left us," I said amused, while waving the sleeves of my white dress in exaggerated gestures. We then went outside, joining a line of young and older men, who walked like obedient soldiers to their posts, as they advanced to dip in the mikvah. We went to a natural source of water, only a short walk outside the village. I was amazed to see all the people walking together in white dresses, taking them off near the water in nature, looking like pure angels, and standing naked like the day they were born. They entered the waterfall and the water pits between the rocks, and immersed their bodies, to the very tips of their fingers, in natural and wild pools of water. My gaze followed as they dipped seven times. The water thoroughly covered every part of their body each time, including the hair on their heads. I did the same as the locals, and connected to the spirit of ascension that was in the water. It seemed familiar to me, but I did not understand how I knew these actions and what they meant. The men who were immersed in the water tuned in their minds to the sun. They turned their gaze to it, to the center of the sky, to the source of life, to the power of fertility and creation, to the sun that charges the body, the soul and the spirit with fresh light and renews them. *How did I know all this about the sun and baptism, without the local people explaining it to me?* I asked myself. My question remained unanswered. I told myself that at the first opportunity, I would ask one of the congregates and seek a spiritual explanation about baptism, and why they make sure to perform it every day before every communal meal. After the baptism was over, the wind and the sun dried our bodies and we put on our white dresses. A short young man about our age approached us and said, "I am John, Miriam's younger brother." We hugged our kin with love. John joined us on our walk back to the village during which I observed how the place operated. It looked to me like a nest of busy ants, a community where its members are connected to each other in their minds and spirits through a series of common customs, rules, and laws, obeyed by all.

The members of the cult work and move in immaculate order, which is governed by the rules of the leaders responsible. Every member I saw, man or woman, wore a white simple garment, and worked in the various crafts according to local custom. Each person seemed to be where they were supposed to be at any given time and acted with strict obedience.

John told us, "I was asked by my sister Miriam to take you to Judah the Elder, a senior leader of the Essene and a learned member of the Council of the Twelve." We went with him to the eldest of the sages, who was expecting us. As we walked along the dirt paths, we passed public buildings and humble cloth pavilions. Judah, the eldest of the sages sat in the shade of a large palm tree on a wooden chair with a high seat, looking like an authoritative king. His clothes were white and clean, his hair and long beard were white, and he radiated light and inner peace. His eyes were hooded, and it was obvious that he was engaged in introspection as we approached him. When we stood close to him, he opened his eyes in an instant, and was alert and attentive to us. He spoke to us authoritatively in high language, a kind of sacred language.

"Peace be upon you, my sons, may peace be upon your souls always. I would first like to greet you on your coming to Qumran and your desire to join our community as the Unity Congregation of Essenes," he said. "As fresh candidates, I will tell you a few things and explain the term under which we live and the expected tests, so that you can adapt yourself to our ways." He spoke these words in a stern and precise tone of voice, then turned his gaze to Nimrod and continued in a tone of reproach and command. From that moment, I noticed that he began to ignore my presence and addressed his words only to Nimrod. I wondered about that, but due to the profound respect I had for his stature as the elder of the sages, I continued to stand and observe him quietly, trying to learn and draw knowledge from everything that was happening. I hoped that I could understand and learn how I could best integrate and contribute. Old Judah continued and said, "We Essenes prefer to withdraw from the people, and do not try to impose our faith over anyone outside of our congregation. We stay away from the pleasures of the body as if from an evil measure, and a great virtue is for us to conquer our desires and not give in to lust. We advocate abstinence and despise wealth. It is our rule that anyone who joins the community surrenders all of their assets to us for the benefit of the entire community.

"A candidate is not immediately accepted. They must wait about three years before they pledge allegiance. Before taking their oath, members of the community provide guidance on our way of life as they get deeply acquainted with the candidate's nature and examine whether they have the ability to govern their spirit and desires. Even after proving this, we continue to carefully examine the individual's conduct among us. If they are found worthy after this process, they are accepted after swearing allegiance to the Togetherness Cult. They must also fear God, conquer their passions, and maintain justice for human beings, without harming others and the commandments of others. Such conduct ensures that those who join our community will remain loyal to our laws and secrets and obey the elders. Our teachings are secret and intended only for the Essenes, meaning only they are allowed to know its secrets after swearing allegiance to the community. Anyone who violates these rules will be immediately ousted. A member who blasphemes, who is rude, who behaves violently or who disobeys the Council and their beliefs will be tried immediately and sentenced to death. Our ways of life are strict and include avoiding family life and women, with the few exceptions. We avoid engaging in trade and focus on farming and crafts. Our daily routine includes prayers, purifying baptisms, shared meals, and work for the greater good of the community. Our members worship God by virtue of their righteousness, honesty, and obedience to the laws of the Torah.

"We believe in the soul remaining forever. Only the body decays and dies. Matter is transitory, but the soul is immortal. When the good soul is released at death, it is filled with joy and rises as if set free, moving to a vast space like an ocean where a pleasant wind blows, as it reaches heaven. However, the evil souls turn to a remote and gloomy corner of creation, where storms of torment wage endlessly. It reaches hell. We believe fate is predetermined by God, and therefore man does not have a free choice in life between good and evil. One must do good without expectation of receiving a reward in the next world. A good person does good because of their constitution and level of development." Old Judah paused for a moment and then began examining me and Nimrod from head to toe, observing not only our physical form but also our inner essence.

He seemed to be looking with his wise eyes around and above our bodies as well, scanning something briefly. After that he turned to me and Nimrod individually and said, "Nimrod, you are destined for leadership, and therefore I will attach you to Nahum the priest, a member of the Council for his guidance. You, Asaf, are destined to be a healer and a spiritual teacher, therefore you will be guided by Asa the priest, who is not a member of the Council. He can teach you balance, healing and wisdom." Old Judah finished his words, then gestured with his head to John to take us away.

I was excited and full of questions, yet worried to see Nimrod's enthusiastic reaction and his face turn red with excitement. He was thrilled that he was chosen by Old Judah to be one of the future leaders of the Essene Unity Congregation. I was troubled by thoughts about fears, and if it would be right for me to become a priest in a sect and give up the chance for a relationship and family life in the future? I thought about beautiful Miriam, and that if I became a member of the cult, I could remain her friend and 'brother,' but never her partner... These thoughts surprised me a lot and I felt a little confused.

Chapter 4

It is morning, and I walk the dirt paths of Qumran on my way to my first meeting with Asa, my teacher. Out of the corner of my eye, I see on the side of the road a vivid acacia tree with a brown trunk and branches, covered in thin green leaves. Among the branches I spot a white-breasted owl hiding, with its eyes closed, sleeping.

The owl is so spectacular that I am not sure if it is real or a figment of my imagination. A few moments go by, and I hesitantly approach a lone tent at the edge of the camp, where I am to meet with my teacher Asa. My heart is filled with excitement ahead of our first meeting, and I am somewhat scared. I notice that a handsome and powerful man with black, graying hair is sitting on a small rug at the entrance of the tent. My heart starts beating with excitement. "Good morning, Asaf," he greets me in a deep voice. "My name is Asa," he adds and stands up. He appears to me as a tall man of about fifty years old, looking directly at me with piercing black eyes.

"I have been waiting for you, Asaf, to share with you the healing secrets of the Essenes, Son of Light I will be able to guide you through the process we all go through, so that you may reach a higher level of spirituality and unwavering clarity. You will undergo purification and inner cleansing; change the way you think and let go of limited beliefs with the help of getting close to nature, the desert, springs, and caves.

"After spiritual cleansing, the members of our community go through learning and awareness processes, dedicated to moving to other dimensions, learning to connect the physical and spiritual aspects of their lives. We learn to enhance the senses and decipher codes imprinted in the spirit from previous life transitions, some of which remained locked up due to past trauma.

"If you pass those stages successfully, you will be transformed and reborn into the divine being within you, and you will be sworn into the role you shall play in the Unity Congregation.

"On my way to you, I saw a white-breasted owl sitting on a tree. What was that owl?"

Asa answered, deeply impressed by my words, "It is the guiding animal of your life's path. The owl came today to inform you of your vocation as a spiritual seer and healer, devoted to the forces of light and purity in the universe. This confirms that I may pass on to you the secrets of the ancient healing order as a warrior of light banishing the forces of darkness, because the owl is my guide as well.

"The owl heralds the existence of a person who is fearlessly loyal to the truth. He is strong and brave. He meets the forces of darkness and knows how to transform them into light. The ability of the owl to see the truth in everything allows him to better control the energy of creation. He distinguishes between light and darkness and each of their roles as forces of creation.

"The owl can carry you on its wigs to other dimensions and bring you back charged with wisdom, magic and abundant spiritual healing capabilities. He will help you reach deep into your core, the inner truth of your being, which transcends all masks, and through it, create magic.

"The physical body of a human being is wrapped in a spiritual shell, called the cloak of light. It is a transparent husk, yet it contains all of the colors of the rainbow. It is in there where the most virtuous healer develops yet another layer of golden light fibers. This occurs when he holds and fully obeys the laws of the universe wholeheartedly.

"The owl you saw is evidence of a spiritual master from the higher worlds, who accompanies you to ensure that your path is protected. He safeguards your path of service and love and demands your total devotion to creation and light.

"A true healer," Asa added, "is a son of light who walks the path of purity, unites all parts of oneself, and maintains that purity. The key is a balanced area of light that runs along the axis of the center of the body and resides in the core of the heart. This, unlike sons of darkness who draw life energy for themselves out of arrogance and selfish desires to control creation and pacify short lived desires and hunger for power.

"The healer builds his strength in purity and in accordance with the rules of creation. He leads himself balanced and true, controlling his energies out of pure distinction. He is led by light and love and the desire to serve humbly and justly. He learns to control all facades of his spirit to fulfill his unique destiny, which is intertwined in the universe as a whole.

"I will teach you how generations of healers build their energy known as the 'chariot,' so that you may channel the cloak of light in a way that creates a space, which gives its owner the ability to shape reality and move in the spaces of the universe, transition between dimensions, stars and skies."

I listened to my teacher, absorbing his wisdom in silence, trying to internalize and understand his complex words without question. After sharing long moments of silence, we parted, but agreed to see each other at dawn at our meeting place, the tent at the edge of the camp, in the secluded and quiet area next to the palm trees. I thought of Miriam, who is also Asa's student. It would be remarkably interesting to discuss with her the processes she is going through, and to share experiences and insights of the inner self."

Chapter 5

It is almost noon. In a short while, it will be prayer time, the time of baptism, of purification in the mikvah by the dining hall, where we will all soon eat lunch together. While I was walking the trails of Qumran, I crossed paths with the beautiful Miriam. She stopped to greet me and said that she was on her way to lead the 'women's generating dance group.'

"We dance on weekdays, on holidays and on the Sabbath. Would you like to accompany me and watch us dance?" I was happy to oblige. I was curious to see the dance no less than I was glad about the opportunity to go with her as I was attracted to Miriam and wanted to get to know her better. We entered one of the buildings intended for gatherings during which the congregation would chant and dance in thanks and praise to God. Miriam said, "In the Unity Congregation, we see ourselves as residents of a temple, and our bodies as a living temple of thanksgiving to God. Instead of making a sacrifice as is customary at the Holy Temple, we express our gratitude to God through songs, chants, and dance. The dancers generate a change in their spirit within themselves and in their surroundings as they create new fields of light."

We entered the compound where women, young and old as one, were waiting for their instructor. Miriam called the 'generators' and herself, "the orphan women who found refuge in the 'Unity Congregation' of the Essenes."

"I initiated meetings where I teach these women sacred dances, just like my mother taught me, and my grandmother taught her before that." Miriam explained. "We pass on and dance the secrets of generating from ancient times through various dances during sacred events here in Qumran. The talent to generate has been passed down in my family from generation to generation of women. I hope that in the future I will also tutor my daughters in sacred dance as part of my maternal lineage, if I get to give birth. These sacred dances, which were originally shared with us by the priestesses of ancient Egypt, use movement to make special geometric formations, creators of harmony, which are the language of beauty and unity in creation. This is a noble way to express unity and praise to the Creator of the world, to the divinity that is in each and every one of us."

I saw Miriam, the leader of the generators, enter the building and greet the dancers who were waiting for her and her guidance in this period before Passover, the festival of freedom. They were waiting to start a dance that they had practiced several times in the last few months. Miriam first gathered them in a large circle, took a few deep breaths, and placed her palms on her heart. The other women did the same. One woman who was standing on the side of the hall began to softly beat a round hide drum, tapping a rhythm with her fingers and a wooden stick with a smooth round end. Another woman, who was standing next to her, began to play a deep tender melody on a wooden flute synchronized with the drum. The melody of the flute reminded me of crying and longing for places far from the world known to us and from our earthly lives. The women of the circle and Miriam started moving in bewitched movements, waving their hands in circular motions up and down and above their heads, and down in a spiral around their bodies. They split into pairs and then joined into trios, moving, and making formations that changed and united with each other. After that, they returned repeatedly to the original big circle formation, from where they started at the beginning of the dance.

The dance lasted quite a while, but it seemed that they were dancing without effort or fatigue at all, and were filled with life energy and joy, and in the process, I, the observer, was filled with those energies as well. They danced barefoot, their hands swaying, holding scarves that moved and flew like angels' wings. They indeed looked divine with their female bodies cloaked in white as they created a gentle dance, surrendering to the whiteness and listening to the silence beyond the sounds. In their dance, they brought about a unique and whole self-expression for all sisters in the circle. I wanted to watch them longer... Their dance gave me a healing that filled me with the power of an eternal presence that suddenly burst within me, towards a multidimensional world of beauty and light. Finally, when the women of the congregation finished their dance, they hugged each other before going their separate ways.

Miriam came back and stood beside me, she looked into my eyes with her smiling blue eyes, expecting my comment on the dance I had just seen. Her eyes suddenly filled with wonder, and she asked, "How did you feel? What do you feel, Asaf?"

I was excited and thrilled, and I told her that I had never seen such a beautiful, spectacular dance, harmonious and full of life. "Your tremendous work with them is sacred, no doubt." I added.

Miriam thanked me and said, "Thank God that you received such an impression, Asaf, and you will surely have the privilege of watching the dances during ceremonies, holidays and various occasions here in Qumran." She asked if I would join her for lunch and walk with her to the dining hall, and I said, "Yes." On the way there, Miriam explained to me that the joint meal is equitable to the custom of offering sacrifices in the Holy Temple in Jerusalem. When we got to the dining hall, I said goodbye to her, and she went to help the cooks and serve the food to the members. She entered the kitchen and I saw through the door open kitchen cabinets laden with glasses, dishes, and jugs. Outside the building, under a palm leaf covered hut, the women cooked the meals in a clay underground oven.

I dipped in the mikveh before the meal, as the local custom commands. The baptisms in all mikvehs symbolizes, as was explained to me, the separation between the holy and the profane. We dipped in the water of the mikveh, and then we changed out of our work clothes into clean clothes. A feast was held twice a day, in the morning and at noon, and it opened with the priestly blessing over the bread and the wine. At every meal, we entered the great hall and sat down on mats woven from palm leaves, handmade by members of the community. We sat along the wall facing each other. Each diner took his place in a fixed seating order, one person leaning against the wall, and the other sitting in front of them with their torso upright. We ate in complete silence, as customary. Nimrod, who was already there, took his place in front of me, but I saw that he was restless. I knew that it was forbidden to break the silence when eating, because the meal constituted a sacred ritual.

We also knew that anyone who broke silence was punished by removal from the dining hall, so I didn't ask him what was bothering him. The meal served by the women of the community consisted of bread and grape juice, dates, porridge, and a drop of milk, which we ate in clay plates and cups, handmade by the locals. I reflected on Miriam's words in our earlier conversation and felt the stillness and silence that prevailed in the hall. I felt that we really are a pure and powerful human substitute for the Temple. We are a kind of "living stones," which replaced the building blocks of the temple. We are the physical-corporeal temple in Holy Jerusalem, and the meal is truly a sacred ritual.

After finishing the meal in complete silence, I went with Nimrod to joint spiritual activities for the men, joint Torah studies and prayer, which continued for many more hours into the night. Members study in shifts, they explained to me later. There are three study groups, and each group studies a third of the night.

This is how a sequence of learning is created throughout the entire night, thus keeping the light of the Unity Congregation shining constantly. I became part of a community that interprets the Bible and writes it as well as sacred textbooks on the paths of wisdom and magic of the Essene sect. At one of these meetings, I heard from the members who wrote scrolls of wisdom in the Unity Congregation, and I asked Asa my spiritual teacher to teach me to write such scrolls as well. I learned that there is also a one-of-a-kind scroll, which rests on a copper leaf. This secret scroll opens with a list of the discovery of ancient treasures and continues with a description of the place where treasures from the Second Temple are hidden, including the Ark of the Covenant, the Menorah and many other holy vessels hidden in caves near Qumran and protected by members of the community.

Nimrod seemed to me to be overjoyed with enthusiasm when we returned from the spiritual activity. I assumed that it was because he had begun his leadership training with Nahum the teacher, who was one of the dignitaries of the congregation and part of the council of twelve. On our way to the cave to sleep for the night, I asked him to share with me his exciting experiences, and he promised me that we would talk about them soon. We ended the day in a quiet and peaceful slumber, except for one disturbing dream, which gripped me and woke me up early in the morning. I dreamed of Miriam. I saw her sitting under an acacia tree at the edge of our camp, cradling a newborn baby girl.

When I approached her, she asked me to bless our baby, born after many hardships. She handed me the baby and said, "Her fate is in your hands." I tried to understand what she meant, and I asked her in fear what hardships we had gone through, but she remained silent. She just continued to stare at me with her big, sad eyes, as she shed tears of sorrow, without sharing with me the reason for her sadness. I woke up from the dream in a panic. What a scary dream indeed.

Asa

Chapter 1

I am currently training a student and a unique 'son of light' named Asaf son of David. I had waited for him from several months as he kept appearing in my dreams, where I learned that I was the one who would become his spiritual teacher once he joined the Essenes. "A great healer is about to come to you," the Archangel Michael announced in one of my dreams and said, "you know each other from your previous transitions in which you had served as his and another kindred spirit, Miriam's teacher.

"You will meet again," the Archangel Michael continued, "to complete a study that you have not yet completed in the transition of your previous lives, and in order to free yourself from old barriers and advance together to a higher level of light."

Therefore, I am hopeful that Asaf will pass the spiritual entry tests so that he may become, in due day, my successor. I am fifty years old, and I have been in the Qumran Unity Congregation for about a decade. I teach and train members of the sect, helping the Sons of Light to fulfill their destiny by self-actualization in the path of light. I also ensure that they behave according to the rules of morality, the spirit, the Torah, and the norms of our group.

When I first came to Qumran from Jerusalem, I was appointed keeper of the Ark of the Covenant, also known as the Holy Ark. The Ark, which is in the hands of the Council of Essenes, is the very one that was given to the Israelites at Mount Sinai, containing the Stone Tablets inscribed with the Ten Commandments.

I was born in Jerusalem, and my mother placed me, when I was just a few days old, in a basket at the doorstep of Eleazar and Deborah, who were among the city's noble class. Eleazar my father, who was one of the priests at the Temple, picked me up after he had rushed out to trace the sound of a crying baby. He adopted me that very day, giving me love, a good Torah education, and I lived like a highborn, as did all sons of high-ranking priests in the Land of Israel. I regretted that I never met my birth mother, nevertheless I felt that she made a righteous sacrifice by giving me up to the family she did. I guess she probably wanted me to grow up in a home where I would acquire an education, a higher social status and better living conditions than she could have given me. Growing up I thought that maybe he was my real father, and perhaps he wanted it to be that way? My adoptive mother could not bear children despite her attempts to conceive until a late age and was so delighted to receive such a long-awaited yet unexpected gift. When I would walk the streets and markets of the city of Jerusalem to buy groceries, I noticed that older women were watching and secretly staring at me. Sometimes I also saw street vendors and women passing by looking at me and then immediately looking down. Perhaps they knew who my birth mother was? And maybe they had to keep what they knew a secret for reasons related to status and social etiquette?

One day, I noticed that a short and thin young woman often watched me, standing in a corner, hidden near a house in the street near the market. A woman who glanced at me with sad, black eyes, then shed tears under her headscarf that hid most of her face, making her harder to recognize. Every time, before I could approach her, she would slip into one of the houses, quickly disappearing from my sight. The mystery surrounding my identity and the secret of my true origin began to preoccupy me from the very beginning of my life, paving my unique spiritual path from birth to my later years. A path where my basic questions are unanswered... and for that I am grateful, despite the pain within me, which I feel less of as I carry out my meaningful spiritual mission. Well, that is the way of the world... the good and the challenging are intertwined. My adoptive father and his fellow priests at the Temple taught me to read and write, Torah, values, and beliefs, and I became an educated man. However, despite the great love and care given to me by my family and those around me, my heart remained restless. The void in my heart sought to know its origin and the woman who gave birth to me.

When I grew up, my parents wanted to marry me off to Ruth, a woman from a good family and of high social status. Ruth was invited to us for a family meal with her parents and at the end of the meal, they left me and her alone in the grape arbor outside our house, so that we could get to know each other before we decided to officially marry. Ruth was charming and smart. She looked at me with her black eyes, full of hope that we would get married, and spoke in a quiet and pleasant tone. I felt that she fell in love with me. Despite her virtues and even though I was captivated by her charms and even secretly fell in love with her too, I decided not to marry her. I continued looking for many years for another woman, who would be a better match for me. However, as the years passed, I felt that there was no woman in whom I could find the impossible ideal that my soul had created. I imagined that I would find a woman who resembled my mysterious ideal birth mother. I came to envision a female figure that naturally remained unattainable, until finally I had no desire at all to marry or have children. Well, so is the way of the world... it sends you back a reflection of your beliefs in an accurate way from each moment.

Later in life I wanted to become an instrument of the Creator and bring wisdom and healing to my surroundings. I finally found my home in the Unity Congregation in the Judean desert. There I taught healing methods and lived simply and modestly, deeply fulfilling the role given to me as an Essene teacher. I became one of the elders of the sect and the guardians of the holy instruments, which are the Ark of the Covenant, the Menorah, and other secret items. I became the guardian of the Ark of the Covenant hidden in one of the caves, known only to me and Judah, the head of the Unity Congregation, member of the Council of the Twelve leading the Essenes. Only we knew the whereabouts of the Ark of the Covenant, and how to apply it. Four times a year, on the two equinox days and the two solstice days at sundown, I walked for about two hours from Qumran to the top of one of the remote desert cliffs and waited for a chariot of fire to come to me from remote stars.

Chariots of fire angels from the distant stars came to meet me and bestowed me with knowledge through codes transmitted directly to me in the form of symbols. Messages and healing secrets are sent to me, and I study them and process them, then pass them on to Judah. As a keeper of the Ark of the Covenant and a priest, I connect the people of the congregation with those angels from the stars who visit with me. I know that the angels come from the stars in a chariot of fire, since the days of Mount Sinai, where they gave Moses and the Israelites the Tablets of Law, which were placed inside the Ark of the Covenant. Every week, I secretly come alone to the cave where the Ark rests, charge my being with its light and powers, and transmit this light to the light grid surrounding the planet "Earth" and to the gate of light located in Qumran. In the coming years, I will begin to train my student, Asaf son of David, in the secrets of the Ark of the Covenant, and how to apply its light in the Land of Israel and Qumran. I will have him work as my curate. I shall train him to succeed me as a keeper of the Ark, who will continue the work once I have passed. I will do so with the utmost care and hope that he will succeed in ascending to the elevated level of light necessary for this mission. I will teach the collection of ancient secrets passed down from our priestly ancestors, and everything that happened at Mount Sinai, where Moses received the first tablets and smashed them. I will tell him about the second set of tablets that Moses went to receive on the top of the mountain. the tablets of the covenant were inscribed with the Ten Commandments for humanity, by which we Hebrews were expected to live according to a set of values and according to high beliefs, and to serve as a living example as Sons of Light to the rest world.

We were chosen to raise light to the dimensions of the spirit and the "higher good," such as the children of the star Sirius and the Pleiades in the center of our galaxy. Our ancestors from the stars, those who sowed the seeds of life on this planet, wanted to add planet Earth to The Seven Sisters – the Pleiades. They sought to turn the planet Earth into a paradise, consisting of a wide variety of creatures, who would be able to specialize the creation and the love for creation within their lives. The tablets made of sapphire and placed in the Ark are not only a set of rules and laws that must be established in society, they are actually a device given to us by the angels, which enable us, among other things, to travel through time and other dimensions. It is a device from the stars, a gateway to the home stars to create a wide communication between the dimensions, facilitating cooperation between humans and races inhabiting other planets. The Ark of the Covenant is made of a gold box with special dimensions, which were known to Moses in ancient Egypt. The cabinet amplifies the light of the sapphire panels, on which are engraved ancient symbols and codes of the constellations. The sapphire panels and the Ark that contains them, transmit light that is used as a protective sphere for the people or community that obtains it. The Ark can also transmit and receive messages that enhance the light aura of its keepers. Its guardians can create journeys to other stars by channeling traffic in these light fields. The Ark of the Covenant radiates light, a radiation so strong it is dangerous for people who do not have a strong and bright light aura. I was asked to guard the Ark, and I was trained for this by the chariot of fire angels who also gave me crystals and buried some of them in the aura surrounding my spiritual body. Can I today carry the radiant fire of the Ark of the Covenant and be charged with it, then transmit and translate its messages to the network of angels of light, which envelops the planet Earth and serves as the universe's "library of knowledge"?

Chapter 2

Today, on the night of the summer solstice, I will go to meet the angels who will be arriving in a chariot of fire from the stars. I had already received a reminder call of this in my mind inviting me to the meeting, and I was asked to come to the top of the cliff at our regular meeting place in the desert. I remember with excitement the first meeting a decade ago, when I first saw a silver ball of fire in the sky which turned out to be the chariot of fire. I was searching for my own path at the time, and I wanted to leave the holy work I was doing at the Holy Temple in Jerusalem. I looked for another vocation, and I turned my hope filled gaze to the sky, praying every day for help from the Creator. One bright summer evening, as I looked up at the sky and prayed for spiritual guidance, I saw a light in the sky twinkling like a star, moving from one place to another quickly approaching, receding, then disappearing all at once. I began to follow the twinkling light, which continued to appear in the Jerusalem sky every night. It began to come closer and appear before my eyes in the form of a ball of a bright silver light and continued to move in the sky and move away until it disappeared. It appeared before my eyes for seven days. Each time I decided to follow and search for its whereabouts, it would disappear. I followed it for about three nights. I rested during the days and approached the place where it vanished, and on the third day when it disappeared from my sight towards dawn, I found myself in the area of the Jordan River. The sun had come up when I met a man who introduced himself as "John the Baptist," and who engaged in the work of purification and bringing people closer to God, by baptizing them in the waters of the Jordan River.

That morning John baptized a large group of people in a ceremony on the banks of the river Jordan. I witnessed the people transform through a deep mental process, after being baptized in the river. They entrusted themselves in his hands, were baptized and born again, full of hope, leaving their past, suffering, pain, and mistakes behind. I spoke with John, and he asked me, "Have you also come to be baptized, to achieve purification and connection with God"? I told him about myself and that I was looking for a new path to my destiny, and that I had come from the Temple in Jerusalem. I also told him about the shimmering chariot of fire that had disappeared, and that I followed it to this place where I met him by the Jordan River. John was terribly moved by my words and said that I had come to the right place, to receive guidance and answers to my mysterious questions. He was not at all surprised by my words about the chariot of fire. A chariot of fire also appeared in front of him and his cousin, and its angels have been meeting with them for quite a while. His cousin is Jesus son of Joseph, whom John called "Messiah the Deliverer."

It was the first time I heard about Jesus son of Joseph, and I asked what he was preaching. "About the end of days and the coming of a new era on earth," John explained. "The Deliverer came to give people tools to live a life of transcendence in the light, and he knows how to deal with the darkness that is taking over our world, that is, to guide us to the Kingdom of Heaven on Earth, which is 'Messiah Consciousness.' The unity is between a person's spirit and body, a balance between spirit and matter, between justice and truth in action. I, John, was destined to announce the coming of Jesus and serve as a close witness, watching and knowing Jesus' ability to guide and perform miracles, as an instrument of the Creator and as His incarnation in this current time."

He added that after he baptizes me in the Jordan, I will undergo spiritual purification and be able to meet Jesus, ask him questions and receive guidance for a new spiritual path for my life. After I accepted John's invitation, I was baptized in the Jordan river, and waited to meet Jesus son of Joseph who was nearby, surrounded by a group of dozens of disciples. I saw women and men sitting in a large circle on the riverbank shaded by trees, listening to his address and receiving his healing. I waited patiently for the end of the sermon that Jesus delivered to the crowd, and I followed him to his tent on the bank of the river. He received me for conversation with generosity and love and asked me to sit next to him in his tent and to treat myself to some water and dates.

I told him about my search for my life's purpose and my calling at this point in my path, and I asked for his spiritual guidance. I continued to describe the revelation of the chariot of fire that brought me to him and to his cousin, John the Baptist. Jesus hugged me lovingly and said, "It is good that you listened to the signs and followed the chariot of light." He wrapped me with compassion and put his hand on my head, charging me with light and love. He gave me a short, powerful message in a soft and soothing voice, "Stop looking for perfection outside of yourself, know that God created you whole, connect with him directly. Even though you do not know who your birth mother is, you are no more damaged than any other person. Perfection is revealed to a person who learns to accept their pain and their lack, and through them one finds the right way for oneself. Believe and unite with a power greater than you, the power of creation, out of acceptance and out of personal responsibility.

"The pain that accompanies us in our lives does not change the core of our being, therefore allow it, the pain, to melt the barriers of your soul, and let the barriers be replaced by strength. The strength to love and accept the things that happen for a reason, even if it is not visible to us at every moment, is good for our growth, for it shapes our soul to a new and higher circle in our journey. The power expands our inner strength and resilience, which can be channeled for ourselves, for our family members and for our human surroundings. Believe with all your heart that guidance and wisdom accompany you even in moments of depression and dark loneliness. You were blessed to grow up in a life of abundance, in the home of parents who gave you love, and you are now ready for a new stage in your development. You are ready to fulfill your destiny, one more step of your life. You are meant to serve God out of love of people and the earth, to provide transforming and healing light."

My tears began to flow from my eyes, and they washed away every pain, doubt, and fear from my heart. I felt extremely relieved and started taking deep breaths. I felt that I had been set free. Jesus continued, "Brother, you are destined to be the spiritual guardian of the Ark of the Covenant hidden in a cave by its guardians, the Essenes.

"Go to the Essenes Unity Congregation by the Dead Sea and look for Judah, the head of the Council of Twelve, tell him I sent you. Tell him about the chariot of fire revealed to you, he will know what to do. Judah knows me and John the Baptist because we stayed with the Essenes for a while in the beginning of our journey. We left the congregation when we realized that the way to realize our destiny was different."

Chapter 3

In the dead of night, I walk again, as I have been doing for a decade, towards the cliff on which the chariot of fire usually lands. Waiting for the glimmer of light from above, entering my sight, and getting bigger and bigger before my eyes. This is the silver chariot of fire in the form of a ball that appears before me. It lands softly and quietly on the flat rock surface at the top of the mountain. The sound of a familiar melody echoes in my head as always, when the door of the chariot of fire opens, and out of it come two beautiful familiar angels who are my family members from the stars. They are wearing a bright light blue garment made of a fabric that I do not know, and they approach to greet me. I kneel in reverence, but they ask me to stand up straight, and tell me that we are family members, and that we are all equal. After that they surround me in a formation, with two of them standing in front of me, and two more angels joining them behind me. The two angles behind me are a younger boy and girl, their faces are radiant with light, their hair is golden, and their eyes are blue and large. They magically create shapes in the air, golden geometric light shapes that produce sounds, and the shapes move in a circular motion, then become spheres with a glowing inner center.

The circles move around us, penetrating through the center of my forehead deep into the middle of my head. They sow codes in my mind, wise keys of knowledge that enter my body. These golden symbols are dimensional doors that open and anchor the gates of the channels, which conduct light in currents of electrical fire. The four angels stretch out their arms to me in a powerful ceremony and send currents of love and harmony to the sound of a familiar melody, which I am unable to repeat, because it is comprised of many instruments. Finally, they return to the chariot of fire and take off from there into the sky until the next time we meet, in the fall equinox. So goes the way of the world... nothing new, and everything is cyclical... I stay for another hour on the ridge, waiting for sunrise, and then start my few hours walk to the cave where the Ark of the Covenant is hidden, to complete my task. Old Judah is already waiting for me, leaning on the side of the cliff. I see him from a distance as a white dot, which marks the entrance to the cave. We enter the cave together, just the two of us. The elder of the tribe, and I am his junior by many years, who is to succeed him. We enter the depth of the cave and continue descending to another hidden level. There, behind a wall, lies the Ark. We stand on each side of the golden casket, facing each other, and extend our outstretched hands over it. The codes of light that were plugged into me by the angels earlier begin to move as fluid energy spilling from my palms onto Judah's hands and body. From Judah's hands, they pour like liquid gold into the Holy Ark. The energy currents charge the Ark with new knowledge, some of which is beginning to become clearer to me. I simultaneously experience insights that come to my mind from the wisdom of the stars. Streams of light emanating from my stomach rise and merge with strands of light emanating from my heart. Different levels of parts of myself are revealed to me, and I see through them the essence of truth and divine love, which continues to expand far beyond the narrow perception of reality. In these moments I understand that light and shadow exist within me too and know that they can be combined in balance, out of acceptance and unity. I connect to the unified light of the primordial creator.

The Codes tell me the story of the land of Earth, which wants to change its reality and transform itself into a higher existence, and about dark forces that have taken over it, and must be transformed into the growth of a greater light. The codes buried in the soil of the Gate of Qumran near Jerusalem and the Dead Sea by angels and by us, the Essenes, are time capsules that will be opened to mankind in another era, two thousand years from now. This will happen when many spiritually awake people raise their light auras and change it into a body of golden light. They will use it to open the time capsules, by their very existence and radiation. The time capsules contain keys to advanced spiritual virtues for human beings. They contain healing abilities, high inspiration, understanding without words through the reading of thoughts and feelings, and the ability to move objects or consciousness by the power of thought and spiritual imagination. Judah and I are now internalizing light through the Ark of the Covenant and passing it through this energy gate, at Qumran in the Land of Israel. We support a reality change that will happen on this earth in many generations ahead, in times when responsibility, stability and perseverance in carrying the light in the heart of their being will be required of human beings. A time when human beings will be able to conduct multi-dimensional journeys and travel through time arising from a powerful personal light. A time when the sons of light will be numerous and strong enough to contain the different versions of reality, without losing their focus on their personal vehicle of light. A time when human beings will develop into the New Person, existing out of self-love, harmony, and peace within themselves and with their surroundings. A time in which they will learn to live with a balance between darkness and light, by choosing between different reality options, and by being able to control them by their own power.

Miriam

Chapter 1

It is now close to sundown, and I am once again making the hour-long walk from Qumran to the stream with my brother John. I love this place, because the waterfalls and the bubbling water help me make serene observations and better understand my life. On our way, I again pass by and look at the pools of water that we, the Unity Congregation dammed, under the waterfall. It is from these dams that the water flows through an aqueduct collecting flood water into the reservoirs in Qumran. We continued walking from the stream to the springs located in the southeast of Qumran, and as the evening fell, we sat by the spring, staring into space. John and I like to chat in that peaceful setting. We talk, listen, and advise each other while also enjoying moments of silence together.

It was not easy for us to move from Jerusalem, where we had lived most of our lives, and it was difficult to lose our mother, who died of a heart disease, not long after she lost her partner, our father. Since then, I have been plagued by existential fears, and the pain of separation from my mother and father sometimes numbs my inner joy. Now, as spring approaches, one can breathe and rest a little, observe the movement of the flowing spring water and set aside all troubles. I practice introspection, as my teacher Asa guided me, as part of the healing process I am currently undergoing. Watching the natural flow of water and allowing the pain, fear and doubts to be washed away in the bubbling water, and released.

Learning to feel and allow my emotions to be revealed to me naturally. Sentiments come and go like waves, from their source until they again disappear. I think of father, who was older than mother, and whom we lost five years ago from lung and joint disease. Mother nursed him on his deathbed, fed him, bathed him, and lifted his spirits. She sang to him there as he took his final breath and returned his soul to the Creator, with much love. When my father passed, his expression was peaceful as he was freed from his long years of suffering. My gentle mother, who was a singer and a dancer, died of a broken heart a few months after that, losing her faith in God and her sense of purpose. Such grave despair. I almost lost all hope when my parents left us. I lost all faith in God in my grieving process. I recall how after my mother's death, I found myself alone in the world with John, having no close family members left around us with whom we were in contact.

I was left alone with my brother in Jerusalem at twenty years of age, single and orphaned, filled with sorrow and pain, bereft of direction, a path or faith, and wallowing in deep darkness. If it were not for John, my younger brother, and the responsibility for him as his only kin, I would have sunk into deep feelings of despair and frustration. However, my mother taught me all the important things that I needed to know to continue developing – to sing, dance, love and heal, even when the worst of everything befalls us or perhaps, especially then. I recall that one day, about two months after my mother's death, while still deeply mourning, I went to the vegetable and fruit market to buy food. There I met our family friend Avraham, the neighbor who had disappeared from our neighborhood for about a year. When I saw him, he looked different from what I had remembered. He was radiant wearing his white clothes and I wondered where he had gone for so many months. When our eyes met between the fruit stands, we each greeted the other and I asked him how he was doing and where he was these days. "I now live in Qumran in the Judean Desert, with the Unity Congregation, an Essene sect of monks. I have come to Jerusalem to visit my mother," he replied.

"What is the Unity Congregation?" I asked.

"It is where people enjoy uniting with each other and with God, living a life of purity and holiness. The Essenes are busy helping and supporting each other and share a common spiritual life." I told him that my mother had recently passed away, and that we had been living alone for several months, seeking the next step in the path of our lives, trying to find new connections with people in the wider community, and I noticed a spark of light shimmer in his eyes. "Would you like me to find out if you can join us by the Dead Sea? We are looking for young men and women who can provide services and support to the community, which is mostly men living as monks. We need cooks, people to do laundry, dancers, singers... Shall I recommend you and your brother John as newcomers?" he said and smiled, because he had known me for many years. He knew my skills as a singer and dancer, and about the tradition of this art that has been passed down through our family for generations.

My mother hoped that I would continue her family's long-standing legacy and mentioned it to our neighbor Avraham many years ago.

I was overcome with joy when I heard Avraham's suggestion, and I hoped that this was the answer to all our needs. I immediately understood that there were monks living there living a life of purity and staying away from the pleasures of the world, so I would not be able to find a partner there to marry. I would surely remain in my loneliness as a spinster until the end of my days, I thought sadly, without experiencing motherhood and love for a man. I replied to Avraham that I was open to the idea, and that I would go talk to my younger brother and prepare him for the possibility of moving to Qumran and joining the Unity Congregation. I preferred this option, because I realized what bleak future would await us if we were to stay on our own in Jerusalem.

Chapter 2

The rippling sound of spring water brought me back from my memories to the present with the peaceful knowledge that I was now experiencing a life of meaning. Living in a community with good people, who find high values and beliefs in every area and aspect of their lives. Today I am going through processes of purification and raising my own consciousness, and self-healing with my teacher, Asa, who helps me release barriers and ancient fears that exist in me from past life transitions. Nimrod and Asaf, relatives on my mother's side who recently joined our congregation, give me new hope. I like them very much. They are like two new brothers for John and me. I gained family members unexpectedly. I have a mental and physical attraction to Asaf, a desire to get to know him and the reasons that brought him to join our community. Asaf came into my life at an unexpected moment, when I had already come to terms almost completely with my role in the community, destined to remain single, to nurse our men and to dedicate myself to a life of dancing and singing in sacred ceremonies and holidays, to cooking and washing clothes for all the members of the monastic congregants.

I gave up wanting to get married. I did not believe that I would ever be able to find a suitable partner. But suddenly Asaf came into my life, and he is a charming young man, who stirs storms in my heart. The sun is now setting and John parts with me as he must head to his evening studies. I ask to stay a few more minutes alone, but a familiar and warm voice appears. Asaf came over and sat next to me. I looked at the fit, handsome man, with his beautiful face, masculine chin adorned by a short beard, and reddish hair almost as copper. Asaf gazed at me with his brown eyes, and we spent a few silent nervous moments before he shared his thoughts with me. I felt that he was talking to me as a continuation of something that we had already discussed in the past, even though that had not yet happened in our lives. It was strange. The dimension of time warped, and I felt that Asaf's being has been known to me since forever. He sparked a conversation, as if we had started it a long time ago.

"Relationships in any period of life are like movement between people who want to know themselves and their hearts," he said. "Each person strives to discover themselves through an encounter with another person. Through a heart-to-heart encounter, our feelings are revealed to us, similar to a deep longing for the source of creation from which we all came, and for the power of love. In an encounter with another soul, longings for its source arises, which in the eternal flowing river of life generates longing for the power of life itself. But when we set out to look for love, we must again look for it first within ourselves, to ponder its meaning in our soul and in the depths of our being. It is from this search we sow a seed of longing that will return to us as love at another time. Sometimes the longing for love is forgotten in cellars of the forgotten, and we continue our journey forward in the world without it, but even then, there is a desire to know love. We walk our whole life on a path, searching for our destiny and the power to create meaning, giving back to the world."

I looked at Asaf, and my heart understood every word. I felt that his words melted my heart, and tears of excitement began to flow down my face. His words touched the depth of my being. I felt I knew the meaning of the search for love in the uncertainty and sorrow in our lives, but unlike him I have been for a long time without much hope of meeting a person to love and to actually love him.

I gazed into his brown eyes as he began to pull me to him, as he picked me up and hugged me softly. He kissed me on the lips for what seemed like an eternity, and we fused with loving warmth, passion, and longing, which ignited love in me. I felt that I had returned to him after an awfully long journey, a journey that crossed this life, sailing here from distant regions. A journey where we had already lived together and where we met yet did not remember where clearly. In our embrace, we transmitted to each other the essence of being in our bodies and souls and further expanded to it. The fire of love was ignited when we crossed over into fields of light intertwined and integrated into each other. Like a swirl of flames of golden light, our desire for each other sought to merge, as our hands touched the other's body beneath our clothes. My white dress fell to the ground and so did his white clothes. We drowned each other in a healing, caressing, thirsty and loving touch. We knew that we would each return to each other despite the sea of forgetfulness. Like an insatiable mad dance, we united, and the sun that was in its twilight slowly set. For a brief and eternal moment, I forgot all the anguish and my gloomy thoughts about a relationship and where it is heading. I felt that I was destined to find my Essene mate despite it all.

Chapter 3

At noon, I go to meet Asa my teacher at our meeting place by his tent, and he asks how I am, and sees me still moved by a powerful experience I had yesterday with Asaf and our act of love. He looks at me with his deep black eyes, sits on a pillow at the entrance to his tent, turns to me attentively, and I begin to share.

"I am falling in love with Asaf, a loving relationship is developing between us. I feel that I have found my life partner, but there is a pain in my heart, and I do not know if this relationship will be the one that will last a lifetime. Am I breaking the rules of the Essenes?"

Asa asked if we could walk together around Qumran, happy that I was sharing but was in no hurry to say anything. His silence calmed me down and gave me positive reinforcement for the developing relationship with Asaf, even if it is probably against community rules. Asa led me to a cave at the edge of Qumran, which he called, 'the cave of the ceremony of purification and remembrance (of past life transitions).'

"Your time has come, Miriam, to recognize your strength, and see what is holding your soul back from fulfilling your destiny happily and completely in the world. Today, you will remember your meeting with Asaf in other life transitions and realize why you are drawn to Asaf and are falling in love with him."

We entered the center of the cave. The transition from the light outside to the darkness of the cool grotto was sharp for me, leaving me alert and prepared. Asa started a small fire, and on top of a contraption that he placed above it was a copper bowl with water emitting the scents of myrrh and frankincense. Incense oils made by the local girls for use in celebrations and rituals sacred to the congregation were now dispersed in the hollow. Asa ordered me to lie down on a mat spread on the ground and to let go of my thoughts completely. I lay down on it and began 'circular breathing,' that is, I took deep breaths into my body and exhaled in a set slow rhythm, as Asa taught me a few months prior, as a tool to move into a state of consciousness that enables experiencing an inner vision.

Asa lightly touched the top of my head with light twisting movements, then placed a purple amethyst crystal on my forehead, and another crystal over the area at the top of my head. He explained to me what crystals he was using and said that they have the power to help me easily connect to my memories from past life transitions and see them vividly. He asked me to focus on the center of my chest and my heart as he placed another rose quartz crystal, a pink love stone, on my chest. He told me that I am protected and that I will see things like a vision outside of my body, myself, and all my past life events from a peaceful, loving and understanding perspective, even if difficult or challenging memories come to my mind.

I entrust myself completely to his touch and begin to be 'drawn' to another place and time just like when a dream begins during slumber. In my vision, I am a young woman, waking up in the morning to the kiss of a warm sunbeam, which dazzled my eyes a little. *This morning*, I thought, *is not like other times*, fragments of memories from yesterday began to flood my soul, and with them a deep joy. *Yesterday we received the great gift of light*, I said to myself. I removed my hands from the soft white fur blanket that covered me and noticed a glowing golden aura surrounding my body and my fingers dancing in perfect harmony. It appears as veils of light, moving around my body. I remembered the words of my teacher, Ankh-Aton, who told us in one of the meetings, "The children of the sun deserve its great gift of light. It will oblige you to create reality in your life in a responsible and positive way. You will have to submit your will and conform to God's laws."

I took my feet off the wooden bed adorned with gold lion embellishments.

At the sound of my awakening, the white silk curtain in my room was immediately opened, and two brown-skinned girls, my maids and companions from an early age, quickly entered with their heads bowed, waiting for my blessing. I entrusted myself to their dedicated care, and small, gold sandals were quickly strapped to my feet, and I was covered in a white dress adorned with a gold fringe, befitting my new position. My black hair was groomed with an ivory comb, and my blue eyes were emphasized with black makeup that gave them a feline look. The perfume of rose petals is poured on my neck drop by drop. It seems that I am ready for the morning service where my friends and I gathered, to hear the words of our teacher Ankh-Aton. Before I leave my room, I walk towards an arched window made of white marble. On the windowsill stands my falcon, Horus, whom I have been raising since I received him from my father as a companion on my seventh birthday. Horus, the falcon with the brown feathers, stands firm on his yellow feet and black claws. He is waiting for the meat that I give him, which I fed him every day, and he would appear in my room twice a day, early in the morning and at sunset.

I skillfully fed his mouth with small strips of meat that were placed in a golden bowl on a table in my room. He let out a long, satisfied chirp, then proceeded to fly into the courtyard to meet his falconry, who lived in our kingdom. While I was walking along the brick halls, my mother, Princess Siria, daughter of King Akhenaten, was waiting for me behind the marble columns, our regular meeting place in the mornings, to hug me and congratulate me on my successful initiation the previous day.

"Isis, my daughter, the new golden aura adorning your body suits you," she tells me. "You will look like a beautiful, graceful daughter of the sun. Just remember, your soul carries grave responsibilities as a teacher of the priesthood acolytes, which you will receive once you have completed your training at Tel El Amarna in Egypt. You are destined to train your students as your teacher trained you... in sacred dances, in poetry, in emotional purification processes, in studies of sacred sexuality and in ascension to the eternal spirit. Adhere to purity, light and justice, my child."

"Why are you telling me this, mother"? I ask as tears begin to flood my eyes.

"Many things you do not yet know, for you are young and tender, but you have been chosen from among many to serve in the holy place and guard the sacred knowledge. Not all the priests in the kingdom want what my father, our king wants. The 'priests of Tut Ankh Ammon' fight openly and secretly, like an angry army without restraint threatening to assassinate our king Akhenaten.

"We – your father, your mother, you, your counterparts, your family, and the older priests in our King's court – we shall keep the pure knowledge and belief in one God, the Creator.

"You too must pass on to the chosen children the knowledge bequeathed to you. I pray for you, may God protect you from impurity, vileness, power, and sedition."

I part with my beloved mother and our hearts beat as one. I kiss her and look into her stunning blue eyes before I rush to the temple. Quiet harp music plays in the background as we gather in a circle for a morning lesson with our teacher. As Miriam, observing the Hebrews, I recognize my Egyptian teacher, Ankh-Aton as Asa my spiritual teacher in my current life with the Essenes as they look exactly alike.

The auras of my friends and mine joined and united into a crown presented to our teacher, who sat as a glowing light in a certain point in the circle. Horus, my twin brother, and fellow student gazing at me affectionately with his clear blue eyes, Horus as Asaf in my current life with the Essenes.

Our teacher began and said, "Today I will speak with you, my sons and daughters, about the engagement ceremony or 'unification,' in which priests and priestesses, that is, yourselves, communicate with entities from planet Sirius, and unite with the other priests in the great pyramid. This is our offering to our ancestors from the stars of the galaxy, and their ancestors, the golden angels who dwell in the great sun, Sirius."

Upon hearing his statement, Horus and I rose to our feet and approached each other, to team up to serve the light in the Great Pyramid. We walked one after the other forming a lengthy line of pairs toward the great pyramid. Our ancestors from Sirius, I reflected... remembering what my mother told me as a child before bed. She loved telling me with such grace about gods and goddesses, our ancestors and our older brothers and sisters from around the galaxy, who love and nurture us, who are living on planet Earth. "We are to them," she used to explain, "like children, as you are to me."

"How do they live, and what do they look like, Mother"? I asked.

"Some of them are like us, strong and beautiful, and some of them look like lions and dolphins. Their bodies are clear and bright light, their wings are white, and their hearts are full of love and compassion for each other," my mother replies. "They live with each other in peace and harmony, and they believe in the one God, the Primordial Creator, as the source of the entire system of creation. They know the essence of the power of creation under God's laws, filled with a sense of love and justice." My thoughts now returned to the line of students marching together behind our teacher to the Great Pyramid.

My thoughts wandered to yesterday when we received the great gift of light. We stood in a large circle, in the center of which stood and spoke our teacher Ankh-Aton. His words replayed in my ears, and my spirit returned to that experience. "The great light, the source of the light in heaven is in your heart," said Ankh-Aton. "The union of the bodies in your being is bathed in golden light, which is purified by a dim light from above."

My heart was beating rapidly with excitement when I heard him speak. It was not the first time I heard these words. I huddled together with my friends, the acolytes, standing in the white study hall with me. I understand these words better than ever before. The soft white linen dress rested on my body, and my bare feet absorbed the chill of the smooth marble floor I was standing on. Twelve selected trainees stood in the morning circle, huddled and attentive to our teacher, Ankh-Aton. Unlike other mornings, this was a special event for us. We knew that today we would receive the great gift of light and the sun would embrace us as the suns bearing holy light. With this gift comes a heavy responsibility, I learned, but also feelings of joy and longing, before which we humbly bowed our young heads. Listening to our teacher's words, we lined up and followed him to the temple of the sacred pool, where we would undergo the water initiation ceremony, for which we had been waiting for many years in training for priesthood. In unison, we walked slowly, quietly, focused. My heart was beating fast. I am Isis, thirty-three years old, the daughter of their Highness, Ankhera and Siria, and the granddaughter of our King Akhenaten. I have been preparing for this day for so many years, but am I ready to say goodbye now to my spiritual childhood, and replace it with a mature veil of holiness? My question echoed inside me yet remained unanswered. Light blue butterflies came and hovered before my eyes in the folds of their delicate wings, spreading a turquoise-gold glow on my face. Did the butterflies come to symbolize a change in my mind? Did they come to accompany me on my last journey, to the clear pool of water? Hesitation filled my soul.

How will the transition to the new reality take place? My classmate, Suri, walking behind me, read my thoughts, placed a soft hand on my shoulder and caressed it lightly. In my mind, accustomed to telepathic conversations, I heard her say to me, "Walk with confidence, beautiful Isis, you have become a woman, complete the circle to the power of light and love."

"Thank you, my dear Suri," I replied to her in my mind. Why wouldn't that be the case? I will ascend in my body and in my soul, as one unit, I will rise to the heights. I will be used for the knowledge of the Creator's Light. There were twelve acolytes in this class, twin flames, and pairs of biological twins. Six girls and six boys. Couples of the same sign of the zodiac. We silently entered the hall of the sacred pool, the white crystal walls shone and shimmered in glorious light like huge diamonds, enveloping us from all sides. At the guidance of the priest Ankh-Aton, we took off the white linen dresses that covered our bodies and stood naked in a circle around the clear pool of water that projected a golden shine. In the center of the pool, Ankh-Aton our teacher now stood beaming with supreme joy as this day had come after years of our training. I walked to the pool, carefully dipping my feet into the chilly water, slowly approaching my teacher. I was surprised when he put his hand on my head and dipped me in the pool. I plunged into the clear and chilly water and returned to the depths of the mysterious existence, hidden in the womb of creation. I heard the primordial sound of existence coalescing in me in complete silence. Suddenly I lost control of my body. I experienced my being rising up into the vast and infinite space, floating above my body that was still submerged in the depths of the water. My soul reached out two huge arms, which opened and expanded the heart of my being into a plain of golden green light, which enveloped me from all sides. Utmost happiness collected me to perfection, pulsating with fullness and harmony. I could have remained embraced in the arms of the Shechinah forever and ever, if not for my teacher returning me to my body, holding my arm, and pulling me back to the edge of the pool. I obeyed his instruction to get out of the water and was lifted, weightless and dripping water, into the white hall. One by one, my friends entered the pool of water and did not take long to leave it, like a strand of shining gold beads on the necklace of our King Akhenaten. Their solid, golden aura adorned their bodies like a shimmering regal crown, whose light shone far into the distance. We were now partners in a new spiritual force, whose meaning we did not yet fully know. With a sense of promise for the future, we retired one by one, each to their abode, to the peace and safety towards which our path was directed.

***

I am walking in the line of marchers, followed by my brother and classmate Horus. His aura envelops me in love and warmth and pushes my body forward. We were on our way to the unification ceremony at the Great Pyramid. In the brick halls, the place where we resided and studied, we went down steep steps, leading us to the depths of the Earth. From there, we passed through a hidden cave into a long underground burrow, which seemed to be a dark and cold corridor.

A weak light emanating from the walls showed us our way. After a short walk, we reached the top of broad marble steps that led us to the other end of the city of the priests. Our teacher shortened our way to the Great Pyramid by using a secret passage that was known only to the handful of priests of the temples and was now known to us as well. We passed on our way over more stairs and entered a side room. Upon hearing our teacher's words, we sat down in pairs on crimson carpets that were scattered in the room. We have begun the work of purification. Purification of our thoughts and feelings and their transmutation, for the purpose of raising frequencies and unifying them, thus beginning the Unification Ceremony, which was expected to take place later in the Unification Room at the top of the Great Pyramid. Horus and I sat facing each other; we began transmitting energies from our hearts and the center of our foreheads to each other. Our minds merged and united. My knowledge then became his, and his became mine, we balanced each other, purified, and charged each other with life-enhancing powers. My powers began to rejuvenate, my heart filled with pure love, waiting like a wellspring of life, to merge with the power of my Creator.

At the end of an hour, our teacher gently placed his hand on our shoulders, signaling to finish the process of transferring energies, to enter the Engagement Room together. Ankh-Aton began to explain, "The structure of the pyramid represents the four faces of God. Each face is embodied in creation and is a living divine law. Each of the three sides of the pyramid stands on the square base. This creates a triangle that embodies the three flames of God's facades. The pyramid is therefore four times three, which is the number twelve. From every point in the universe, God is revealed in a form multiplied by four, which are the four elements: fire, air, water and earth. The earth receives the twelve-fold radiation of the four faces of God from space, from the planets surrounding it, which we call the zodiac. The sun is the source of light through which the earth receives life energy, in addition to the energy it receives from the zodiac." When our teacher beckoned us to enter the sacred room, Horus extended his hand to me. It was the first time we were given permission to join the secret ceremony, which is performed by the twelve elder priests, among them our teacher Ankh-Aton, who were our other brethren, pairs of twins and biological siblings of perfectly complementing star signs, who were waiting for us in the Great Pyramid.

In front of the entrance, a large round emerald stone platform, with a deep, dark green color, was revealed before me, right in the center of the room. Around it stood twelve circular devices, and in them lay large, transparent, rod-shaped crystal generators with pointed ends.

We were instructed to approach the stage by our astrological signs. Our teacher taught us in the past that the twin pairs of priests are beings with kinship and spiritual similarity, and have the ability to enhance and balance life processes and energy in a bonding ceremony. The priests, who were trained to serve as pairing officers among other things, are a result of planned and engineered pregnancies and births. These are seeded lives that are targeted, planned, and coordinated for a purpose or initiative created by our king Pharaoh Akhenaten. We are a group of people, old and young men, and women, who are twin flames, that is, we were born on the same day, in the same year, and we are all now partners in the holy work. Together we constitute a spiritual amplification force in our work. Now Horus, my brother and myself, Leos in birth, approached the device engraved with the lion. We took out of it two large crystals, corresponding to our star sign. The others did the same according to their horoscopes and began to work with the crystals in pairs. After telepathic instructions were given to us from our teacher, we began. Horus pointed the tip of the crystal in his hand to my heart, and the crystal charged with my life energy began to emit lightning bolts and change its colors to alternate shades of blue, green, and gold. After a while, we took turns, our hands holding the crystal and pointing its tip towards our partner's heart.

The crystals began to change shades to red, orange, and yellow, shifting until their color stabilized at purple blue. We knew this was a sign for us to return them to the circular fixture on the green stone floor in the center of the room. All the other priests did as we did. About twenty-four of us were in the pyramid, twelve young and twelve older priests. At the end of the pyramid ceiling in the room stood a huge sheer crystal generator, which was now absorbing the energies from the twelve energy-charged crystals. We were present at a spectacular sight, where from all directions of the circle violet-blue rays came out and concentrated into the main generator that stood high above the wheel with the smaller crystal rods below it. It began to change its sheerness and became sparkling like a golden diamond, in which flashes of light flickered in a phosphorescent green hue. The glows of light began to weave colorful shapes floating throughout the room. These magnificent symbols and luminous geometric shapes filled the entire hall with iridescent light, accompanied by the increasing divine sounds of violins and harps.

Like tributaries, the sounds culminated into a vast and great ocean of the love of the light. Time stood still. The vast space disappeared, drawn into a hidden gate that suddenly opened out of a great nothingness. Time was also sucked into the great void from which everything was created and returned to it. Light rushes to its Creator like a baby to its mother's lap, and Shechinah's kindness collects it into her arms, like a child returned from afar with immense longing and endless love. As the melody began to slowly fade, like the flapping wings of a departing eagle, the sounds withered away. Then the light was collected into the space of creation, and with it all the knowledge contained in our being was stored away and returned home to the source of the higher faculties in the sun, and a deep silence prevailed. It seemed to me that I had given all the energy I had in me. Like the vessel was empty, and yet miraculously I experienced the feeling of life-filled freshness and renewal. As soon as the ceremony ended, we were ordered to leave the Great Pyramid. We are forbidden to be in the midst of high energies of such excessive intensity. It was the right time to return to our abode in Tel El Amarna.

Chapter 4

I began to wake up from the vision of remembering the transition of my previous life in Egypt, when Asa began touching my shoulder and arm, saying my name in his deep voice, and calling to me, "Miriam, Miriam." He asked me to return with my consciousness to my body and fully come back to the present. I slowly sat down on the mat in the cave, took deep breaths, and was still in a timeless dimension, fully charged with the experiences of remembering. Asa, who sat down close to me, gently asked me if I wanted to ask him anything that would clarify the experience of remembering my Egyptian past. I understood that he knows and remembers that he was my teacher, and that Asaf was Horus my brother, my kindred spirit soul in our Egyptian past in Tel El Amarna during the times of King Akhenaten.

I smiled at him and asked, "What was the purpose of the engagement ceremony we performed in the Great Pyramid on the emerald platform"?

Asa replied, "The ceremony opened an interdimensional gateway for communication with advanced stars and was performed to transmit and receive spiritual information and encrypted energy secrets. The sharing of information between stars is intended to create a high frequency on planet Earth for its development, through the 'light engagement network' that encompasses everything living like a garment made of light, referred to as the Universal Library of Knowledge.

"This is a network of light built from gold fibers with different geometric shapes, which affect the field of the Garment of Light of humans and all living things. The network was created by angels and entourages of light millions of years ago from symbols that are a language that affects your development like a prayer and a blessing. These fibers of light and symbols are the language of the Primordial Creator. They transmit and receive knowledge from distant stars in order to elevate the development of souls to the purity of God. Each symbol belongs to the Library of the Sun in a direct link, and it supports the change of our Garment of Light, its transformation and growth.

"Priests from the past, like you Miriam and like Asaf and Nimrod, can in this life as Essenes revive the knowledge through your body and your Garment of Light, if you remember it and choose to do so. You are destined to do this as a continuation of the knowledge of the secrets of healing and creation, which you gained in your past life in Egypt, and to continue strengthening the light and its ascension in the Primordial Creator's design of love, which is transforming darkness, as part of the service of the Primordial Creator and his purpose in creation.

"Your presence today with the Essenes is the continuation of the realization of the knowledge that we derive from the source, and the transformation of the planet Earth into a high school of love. Planet Earth joins the Seven Sisters, which are stars in the center of the galaxy; a cluster of a thousand stars in the sector of Taurus, and becomes the eighth sister, who will raise the entire galaxy to the power of ascension to a higher octave in the Primordial Creator's light spiral for this universe. That is why we are all meeting again - you, Asaf, Nimrod and I - and this is our destiny."

I was left amazed by the power of the memories and the knowledge that flooded inside me, and I understood why I am attracted to Asaf and have fallen in love with him. I feel that I have known Asaf since forever, and that we continue the communication that started between us in another life. But why do I still feel the pain weighing on my heart? What is the barrier that Asa spoke of, which I must release from my soul in order to fulfill my destiny? This question continued to echo inside me, unanswered.

Chapter 5

A few weeks have passed since my recollection experience of my life as Isis, the Egyptian priestess. I now return to Asa my teacher this morning with many questions, seeking answers.

When I arrived at Asa's tent to continue my studies, he welcomed me warmly and asked, "How are you now, Miriam?" We sat down on a cushion at the entrance to his tent shaded by palm trees, and I felt at home again, encouraged and supported by my teacher. I asked about the relationship between Asaf and I, and what is the nature of the relationship between us in this life. Is this a partnership for a spiritual vocation or perhaps a matrimonial life ahead of us? Asa replied, "Healing relationships sometimes exist between spouses or between partners and friends who respect each other as they are and do not try to change one another. In these relationships, they provide understanding, support, and encouragement to each other, without trying to solve their individual problems. Sometimes Problems arise, but such difficult feelings are short-term, because they are willing to forgive, and because there is a connection of hearts that allows them to accept the difference, without taking the other's mistakes to heart. In such a relationship, it is possible that the souls knew each other in previous life transitions. Kindred spirits have the same light vibration shade because they were created at the same time, similar to biological twins. They are not dependent on each other in any way. As souls, they are neither male nor female, but they are definitely drawn towards each other as soulmates.

"The goal for twin souls is to facilitate joy and creativity. They meet on the plain of unity, or when they ascend to this sphere. This occurs when we recognize ourselves and the God within us, within our lives in our odyssey, which is the journey home and the return to one's whole self.

"At the beginning of our lives, when we leave the unifying light of the Creator, we suddenly encounter light as well as darkness, that is, we encounter the fragmented reality of planet Earth, and experience ourselves as part of the whole. In the intersection between the kindred spirits, we are accompanied by someone who is equal to us and resembles us the most. The connection withstands any separation. Because you have both embarked on a long journey and experienced the difficulties of separation in your life, you get to meet your soul mate.

"In it, you recognize a very deep part of yourself and as a result, you begin to be more aware of who you really are. This encounter can free you from the limiting beliefs that you have adopted in this or in another life transition. You free yourself when you see your reflection in your soul mate. This is a reminder, but it has nothing to do with emotional dependence.

"Meeting your soulmate helps you become aware, and helps you express your creativity and love on this earth. It accelerates your return home, and helps you rise to a higher level of unity. And this, along with preserving your uniqueness and its expression in your life. Each and every one of you is supported by creation and the Creator, while maintaining your individual uniqueness. You must remember this. The kindred spirits remind each other of their essence and accelerate each other towards self-development and understanding the knowledge of unity that prevails in creation. By finding each other, soulmates naturally create something new, a third energy. This energy intensifies awareness and unity within them on a larger scale, and by doing so they also anchor the love and unity within planet Earth by applying their unique skills and talents.

"There is, as mentioned, a deep inner connection between kindred spirits. They create love, joy, and opportunities to enhance creativity and self-fulfillment. They support each other, without falling into the trap of dependence or emotional addiction. Their love turns each into creators of something new. They become a unified third force, in the sense of a positive healer."

Nimrod

Chapter 1

I cannot recall such exhaustion and excitement as I am feeling now since joining the Unity Congregation. I could hardly keep myself from falling asleep during my session with my teacher, Menachem, earlier today. Menachem has been teaching me about the four archangels Michael, Gabriel, Uriel, and Raphael as part of my leadership training. As I head to lunch, I think that it must have been three days since I heard about swearing in angels with the Unity Congregation and today, I have decided to swear in Gabriel and his dedication to enhancing my spiritual strength, will and faith. I have watched as Menachem and other members did this numerous times before and since I have learned that Gabriel can be sworn in too, I have known little rest, though I do not know why.

Lately I have had a tough time sleeping at night, and what concerns me is knowing how I can harness this power for one purpose. My goal is to secretly gather the young people of the congregation and lead them to worship God together and with the help of the Archangel Gabriel. Gabriel, as my teacher Menachem explained, stands facing north before the honorable throne guarding it against the troubles indicated by the prophet Jeremiah "From the north shall disaster break loose." Archangel Gabriel has the power to make judgments on those who deserve them and to save other people through miracles. "Gabriel's voice is like the sound of many waters, and the earth shines through him," said Menachem many times throughout our meetings.

He is able to perform the miracle of saving the People of Israel from their enemies, by virtue of his protective powers. Last night, I had a dream in which Gabriel appeared to me dressed in cloths tied in a golden sash. His face was glowing, and his eyes were red as fire torches. His arms and legs are shiny copper, and his thundering voice heralds the coming of the Messiah. Archangel Gabriel told me that the Messiah was born a long time ago in the Land of Israel and has the ability to teach humans to rise above injustice and evil in our world. "Now gather the young people of your age," Gabriel said, "and give them instructions and ideas, as Archangel Gabriel's messenger." I woke up from the dream covered in cold sweat and excitement, my bones shuddering. It is clear to me that I must gather the youth of the congregation, and this thought does not let go of me, like a disturbing mosquito that buzzes in my mind relentlessly. I will ask John, my cousin, to help me with the task of gathering the youth of the Unity Congregation. John, who is also close to me in spirit, will surely agree. Of that, I am sure. John also established connections with the youth of the community, in which he has been living for quite some time, and he even managed to acquire their trust. My goal is to collect a group of about twenty young warriors of light, and with them prepare for the mission with which Archangel Gabriel will task us. The angel will strengthen our faith every time we pledge our spiritual goals, and together with him we will build our community's brave army of warriors of light. I will now go to meet Asaf and share my mission with him. I will ask him to help me and be my right hand. As my deputy, he will be the gatherer and unifier of the circle of young people within the circle of adults, which we will create together. I will first go to talk to Asaf and share what I have been going through these past days of turmoil. I noticed he felt my restlessness and that he knows about my troubled, sleepless nights, but he does not know of my plans.

Chapter 2

My thoughts are plagued with unrest. I want to talk in a distant corner of Qumran with John our cousin. When I saw him returning from a dip in the mikvah, I approached him with an earnest glare, trying to hide my enthusiasm from him. With earnest effort, I whispered my words quietly and shared my plans with him. I then embraced him at length as if to lock a deep secret. Although he didn't tell me much, I just wanted him to think about things, and I am convinced that he would join me in the group of young people, who initiate acts under the guidance of Archangel Gabriel. During lunch, right after dipping in the mikveh, I stared at Asaf, signaling him to come and talk to me at the end of the meal. When we finished the meal, I retired with him to our cave, where we discussed my situation. Asaf, who read me with great understanding and knew me well, said when we got to the cave that he wanted me to share with him what I was going through these past few days. I shared my experiences with him.

I began by saying, "I have been deepening my knowledge of leadership with the help and guidance of my teacher Menachem in our daily private sessions. We talk and make progress studying, and we engage in dialog on various matters. I learned that the organizational structure of the Unity Congregation was created to serve its needs and desire to obey the laws of the Torah. Ensuring the continuity of living in sectioned classes, initiation ceremonies of members were created, and severe rules of purity and holiness were set in place to prepare for another time in the world, known among Essenes as the 'end of days.' The 'end of days' is a time when the 'sons of light' will live on planet Earth in harmony with the divine plan in creation, in a sort of paradise of peace, balance, harmony and love. This is the reason why clear instructions were also composed in the Unity Congregation regarding property and conduct. The administrative structure usually admits members to the congregation, and the initiation ceremonies are designed to clearly differentiate between those who belong to the group and those who do not. My teacher Menachem told me that there is a huge library in one of the Qumran caves and the most important writings stored in it is the holy Bible. That is why some our rules are so strict, for example the prohibition of laughing, the prohibition of walking naked throughout Qumran, the prohibition of going to the toilet on the Sabbath and the prohibition of interfering in one another's conversation. In addition, abstinence from sex and renouncing marriage. We are not allowed to eat food that is not created within the congregation, and it is also customary to burn the dishes in a furnace for reasons of purity, and to make new ones quite frequently. As you know, Asaf, every meal we eat becomes a religious ritual of purification, prayer and wearing special, white, clean clothes each time.

"The priests of the House of Zadok are the historic founders of the sect and are its spiritual leaders. The Zadok family, I was told, was a noble Jewish family and its sons were priests of the Holy Temple of Jerusalem. The Sons of Zadok believe that the priesthood was given to their ancestors by God at Mount Sinai, and that they were the offspring of Aaron, the brother of Moses. That is why the privilege of the priesthood was granted at Mount Sinai, to the eldest son of Aaron. The Sons of Zadok priests spiritually determine the way of life in the Essene sect through rituals, punishments, and a clear set of rules.

"My teacher, Nahum, told me that a war will break out between the 'sons of light' and the 'sons of darkness,' and that there will be warriors who will fight together with the holy angels and God against the men of darkness."

Asaf asked me, "Who are the 'sons of light' and the 'sons of darkness?'"

"The universe," I said, "was created in advance by dividing into good, which is light, and evil, which is darkness. At the same time, human beings are divided into those who are born to be 'sons of light' and those who are born to be 'sons of darkness.'"

"Therefore, Nimrod told me, we do not have free choice, and each person is destined to a predetermined fate. However, the creative process that gave birth to creation is not perfect, because it suffered flaws. There are angels, who are spiritual beings, which come forward to assist God the Creator in realizing the creation of the universe. The angels were made on the first day of creation, to continue assisting the Creator in His creation of the universe. These angels, called 'Irim,' have adapted to themselves independent desires that do not coincide with the divine plan of creation, and this caused flaws in the process of the creation of the universe.

"These angels mingled with the daughters of men and gave birth to their offspring. This distorted the initial plan of creation. Evil spirits were created from them, and after them, destructive creatures that wreaked havoc and destruction on the planet. This deviation and error obliged God to make a correction, like a flood or annihilation by fire, which killed all life on earth.

"The deity created a correction by destroying the angels, but broke the boundary between the spiritual and the earthly, which happened due to the sin of the angels, and caused a by-product, which affects the human race to this day, and it cannot be undone. That is, these faults and corruptions caused cosmic disasters, which affect the existence of the human race. As a result of this cosmic fault and the breaching of the spiritual boundary to that of humanity, it had a negative effect on the human race, which resulted in the destruction and corruption of God's original intention, as stipulated in the laws of creation.

"The members of the Unity Congregation know the negative by-products that resulted from the sin of the angels," my teacher Menachem explained to me, "and they are engaged in learning ways to overcome them so that they may fulfill God's original intent, and thus support the creative process of creation. When the war between the 'sons of light' and the 'sons of darkness' will materialize, we, the Essene priests, will fight alongside God's angels. God will destroy all the inhabitants of the planet except 'the sons of light.' This will be the fulfillment of the prophecy of the end of days. The sons of light will build a new and pure temple in Jerusalem and will rule the world and lead it from there on out."

"The Essenes believe that the recognition and understanding of the laws of the universe will allow them to avoid the negative effects of that 'mistake' that occurred in the creation process, and thus reach spiritual perfection and the realization of God's will. As members of the congregation, we volunteered to join out of our own free will, which is why Asaf, this is so puzzling to me. These things point, in my opinion, to an internal contradiction, because how can the people of the Unity Congregation say that we are volunteers, after all our work or our dedication has been predetermined for us from the beginning of our creation and our destiny as 'sons of light.' Is man unable to achieve perfection by his own strength? Does the will of man not exist within him directly and act freely for his own sake?

"I would like to share with you, Asaf, my initiative to convene a group of young people from the community and talk about our mission as Warriors of Light and our purpose as young people in the community. I have already spoken with John, our cousin, who promised to think about my thoughts and perhaps bring young people to such a meeting with us following our conversation. Would you agree, Asaf, to be my right-hand man in this initiative of 'warriors of light'?

"Menachem the teacher claims in our conversations that a person's will is not enough to achieve perfection, therefore the member of the congregation must accept laws and rules, and swear by them as part of them being members of the sect, that is, to accept God's will fully, and to align his own will with the will of the creator, to try with all his might to help the power of God's will into the world.

"Man's only choice, therefore, is the realization of the will of God. Hence the circumstances of a person's life are determined by a system of laws that he cannot control. By recognition of the laws in the role of man in the world, a member of the Essenes can adapt his will to the will of God, and thus realize his purpose in the world, achieving spiritual perfection.

"I do not think that is the truth as we do have some freedoms to choose according to our free will and we can create with God. This is why I am initiating a gathering of the young warriors of light."

Asaf listened attentively and was astonished by the knowledge I shared, which was all new to him. "Menachem explains this with great reasonable logic, but you Nimrod, raise challenging questions that are even more interesting." Asaf said. "You raise the questions and doubts you have in your own way and study them in your own unique way without taking for granted beliefs and rules you previously heard about from other members of the congregation."

Before our conversation came to its end, Asaf told me another thing he felt important: that I should talk about it openly with my teacher Menachem and share with him what is bothering me, namely this initiative. It would be worth finding out if such activity is acceptable and allowed under the congregation's strict rules of conduct. I did not answer but through my silence I saw that Asaf, who knew me so well, recognized danger, and he was worried about my future actions and what their consequences could be.

Chapter 3

Asaf, his teacher Asa and I sit together on the ground at the entrance to Asa's tent which Asaf refers to as "The tent at the end of the camp." Tomorrow, Asaf and I will be sworn in by the council at the ritual "Confirmation Cave" after which we will officially become members of the Essenes.

This is the first time since I moved in with the Essenes that Asa asked to meet me face to face and talk to me. I wondered if the reason was the confirmation ceremony and if it was a final test after which Asa would report to the council elders if I was worthy. I was curious about Asa, whom I did not really know personally. I looked at him, and he looked at me back with a piercing glare. I agreed today to join an introductory meeting with Asa, at his request, with immense joy. I just asked myself why Asa wants to hold such a three-way meeting since he is not my official teacher. When I asked Asa the reason for our meeting today, he answered me curiously that it was because he wanted to observe the interaction between Asaf and me, and that this was important regarding a fateful event that might take place in the future. An event that may profoundly change our lives. Asa introduced himself and began to ask me questions. "Do you feel good in the Unity Congregation and with Menachem"? I answered openly, and with vigorous enthusiasm, that the simple life in the sect is good for me, and that the topics Menachem talks about are comforting and challenging and practical, for example, discussions on the place of the individual within the congregation, and one's social affiliation. "True harmony," I said, "comes from a balance between the power of the individual and a greater power, and that I hope that the Unity Congregation will be a home to satisfy both aspects I mentioned."

Asa listened in silence and with a look that was partly in this dimension and partly in hidden realms that only he could understand their meaning. He looked at me and at Asaf with a stiff upper lip. In my heart, I already understood that Asa's silence carries with it a secret that he does not choose to share with me, but I felt that he holds a warm and positive attitude towards me, as he watched and listened carefully to what I had to say. Finally, he said, "The Unity Congregation is like a beehive. The bees work together to create 'spiritual honey' as a work of thought. The bees work out of their own unique place subject to a set of rules that secure harmony and balance for the entire community. A bee realizes itself fully after proving its commitment and perseverance. It approaches honey production with joy and commitment, perseverance, and teamwork. The bee learns to act out of a sense of obligation without violating orders.

The community's royal residence is reserved for the Queen Bee who maintains the continuity of the hive and its fruit, and since she alone gives birth to life, without her, the hive would not enjoy longevity as a productive and shared enterprise.

"This interplay and this sharing exist as long as obedience to the collective laws is maintained. When individuals adopt these laws, they are prepared to give up something for the greater good. When the individual is not fully invested in this delicate and thoughtful balance, or when one feels himself opposing the legality high up in the hierarchy, this structure will find it difficult to contain them, thus jeopardizing the integrity of the entire system."

Asa stopped speaking and looked at me thoughtfully, trying to gauge how deep his words had sunk in. I was incredibly surprised by what he said, and wondered in my heart why he used the beehive and honey imagery. How did he know to read me and see that event that Asaf and I experienced as children related to bees and honey? I realized that Asa was right, because since we were children, I wanted to take the honeycomb at all costs instead of working to create it as part of the teamwork in the hive. Is Asa trying to make me aware of the tension that exists within me and the mistakes I might make because of it? He illuminated in me the tension and the contradiction between the desire to belong to the values and the human family as a group, and my desire to achieve personal gratification of my personal desires at any cost, independently, separate from the group. When the conversation with Asa ended, I went on my way, without thinking about it any further. He brought up unpleasant things that I have no interest in thinking about and feeling right now. Asaf was left alone with his teacher. He later shared their conversation with me. Asa told him as I went my way, "Evil is not a force separate from good, and it exists in our real world. It is not an illusion. The denial of the existence of evil is as false as the belief that there are two separate forces, good and evil. Human evil can first appear as emotional numbness, or as an attempt to protect ourselves from pain and the lack of a loving relationship in our lives. It can often develop into an emotional numbness that continues to exist without a good and just reason. A person who denies evil within them or in their world, becomes cruel to the people around them in a disguised way, which leads to selfish behavior that remains unnoticed.

"There is an ancient legend that ages ago, the land of Sodom and Gomorrah was blessed with exceptional produce from its fertile soil. The Sodom apples that grow in our area of the Judean Desert near the Dead Sea also stood out among their wonderful fruit. Sodom apples were large apples, beautiful and flavorful. The people of Sodom were wicked and sinful, and God sent his angels to destroy them, raining sulfur from the sky, turning cities upon their inhabitants, and the Jordan plain and all the trees and plants of the earth. "Only one tree was left, known as the Apple of Sodom. Its fruit appeared pretty but when opened, they were dark and filled with dirt. When held in one's palm, they disintegrated as smoke and dust.

This is the great gunpowder, which gradually renews itself in fruit. This is an eternal warning to sinners, so that they do not forget the fate of the people of Sodom and Gomorrah, and about such a fruit it will be said,

'On the outside it may be bright, and on the inside, it shall be dark and filthy.'

"In reality, therefore," Asa added, "There are two situations. Bad that looks bad, and bad that looks good. Bad that looks bad, less of a problem since it can be avoided. Evil that looks good, not only are we not wary of it, but we are drawn to it. And here lies the danger. As in the case of the great desert wick tree, which looks spectacular in its vivid colors and shape, its fruit is idle, with thin white fibers and black seeds." After Asaf finished sharing with me what Asa told him in private, I told him that I hope to be a good leader in the Unity Congregation. I want to set an example and lead the future generation out of the values Menachem mentioned – fellowship, truth, justice, love, and mutual assistance. I was happy to meet Asa, and grateful for the fact that Asaf gained such a learned and wise teacher, who teaches him and wants to direct my life as well now, even though I did not completely agree with him. I thought that Asa and the elders' basic assumptions required change, and that the time had come for the young to convey a new message to the adults and to rebel against the rigid and long-standing traditions.

Chapter 4

Today we set off to the confirmation and swearing-in ceremony, ending my and Asaf's three-year trial period as candidates to become full-fledged members of the Essene sect. We put on clean white clothes after our morning dip in the mikvah and had breakfast. This morning we were asked by our teachers to come to the Confirmation Cave at the edge of the camp, where sacred rituals are performed in the ways of the priests. Asaf and I walked together in silence and excitement, with the feeling that the covenant was also between us as partners in the journey, commitment, and choice in our personal friendships as well as our membership in the Essene sect. As we walked, we noticed a writhing viper snake, adorned with brown spots, moving swiftly along the side of the road towards the edge of Qumran. It vanished into the rocks, looking for refuge from the hot sun. The snake symbolized for me the message not to go back but to always move forward and develop with renewed strength. At the entrance of the cave, I noticed strong incense scents of myrrh and frankincense familiar from rituals held on Saturdays and holidays. I also knew the feeling evoked by the intense fragrance from previous events I had attended, a scent of calmness and security. I was ready for the ceremony, and I had a foggy and purifying feeling, elevating the spirit to a high and holy sphere of light. As we entered the somewhat dark cave, my eyes began to get used to the small light provided by the white wax candles, which this time did not smell like honey. They ornamented the corners of the cave and its walls and created shadows everywhere and on our faces. In the center of the cave stood Judah, the leader of the council, wearing a white tunic. He asked us to join and spread his arms wide like a father gathering his children home from faraway lands. We were asked to kneel at his feet. From where we were, his towering face and receding forehead radiated light, and his white beard gleamed. His hands and long fingers beckoned us to come closer and bow our heads. We lowered our heads and placed his hands on each of our heads. Total silence enveloped my heart, and my breath was taken away. Judah began whispering spells in Aramaic in a pleasant melody known only to him. Every once in a while, I could recognize a clear word such as "holy," "God," "armies," and "one"... then: "Holy, holy, holy! The LORD of Hosts! His presence fills all the earth!"

The spells gradually turned from a soft melody to a decisive command full of power, enveloping my body and penetrating to the depths of my being. Judah asked each of us to say individually: "I swear to uphold, cherish and respect the rules of the Unity Congregation, and its secrets that will be given to us from here on and forever." After we said "Amen" together, he replied "Amen and so, may it be His will, our God, the one true Creator of the world." It seemed like time stood still, while all we could hear was pure silence in the cave.

When Judah asked us to stand on our feet and leave the cave, it seemed unnecessary to me. I wanted to stay wrapped with love and a sense of belonging in the peace and tranquility the cave offered. Judah instructed us before we went on our way to retire from all tasks and work for the rest of the day as we would on the Sabbath - to dedicate the time to ponder, internalize and experience things quietly. As we got out of the cave, a blinding light met our eyes. Asaf looked pensive, perhaps because he experienced a deep elation, a sense of belonging to the place, to the new status, to life in the Essene community. I, on the other hand, left the cave straining... Asaf went his way, hurrying to meet with Asa to share his experiences, without paying attention to my struggling feelings, and I asked to go elsewhere to find solitude for the rest of the day.

I remembered the viper I noticed before the confirmation ceremony today, which I saw as a harbinger of an important private message. I kept thinking about what it symbolized to me. I started to climb to the top of the cliff near the camp, I walked slowly and went up the mountain to a secluded spot, from where I can look out on this spring day onto the beautiful expanses of nature. On the sides of the road, there were a few green bushes that adapted to the harsh desert conditions better than I did. I quietly passed by a Sodom apple tree casting shade, but my heart was restless. Finally, I sat down next to a large rock, and leaned my back against it. I watched the arid and pure landscape visible from the top of the mountain. The temporary pleasure and relaxation suddenly gave way to a sharp, stabbing pain in my leg in the shin. I let out a loud cry, placed my hand on my aching shin and managed to see the viper snake that had bitten me moving slowly in a curling motion, slipping quickly between the mountain rocks and bushes. I quickly realized that I had moved away from Qumran, that my life was now in danger and that every moment was now important for my salvation. I rose to my feet with great difficulty and began to drag my bitten right leg. I went downhill from the cliff I had climbed, uttering a curse, another sigh of pain, until I slowly made my way to Qumran. From a distance, I saw the date trees in the village and a few fellow community members standing next to them, carrying bags made of date branches, collecting the crops as part of their work. I let out a loud shout until three people rushed to help me, leaving the baskets of dates on the ground. My friend Simon, whom I knew from our farming work, asked me what happened to my legs. I shouted that a snake bit me up on the cliff. I felt awfully bad and collapsed on the ground. Four of my peers picked me up and began walking with me quickly to Asa's tent at the edge of the camp. My leg began to swell quickly when we met Asa in his tent, and he instructed them to lay me down on a mat inside the tent. I was surprised to learn that Asa's tent was much bigger than it looked from the outside, and I wondered if I was hallucinating from venom that had spread through my body, or if this was what a wizard healer's tent looked like. I continued to scream intermittently, struggling to overcome the pain, until Asa realized what it was about and started bringing medicinal plants from around his tent. He asked for Miriam, whom he had trained in herbal medicine in recent years. Miriam rushed into the tent after a few moments with great worry. She had bowls of clay and herbs in her hands, which she began to crush and mix with olive oil, while speaking soothing words to me, and explaining to me about the plants and their names, and their healing effect on snake bites, trying to keep me awake and conscious. She mixed herbs and said aloud: "Thyme, moss, wormwood, frankincense with olive oil," and created a fresh paste. Then she boiled water outside on a fire and poured herbal tea from sharp varthemia and desert white broom and made me sip the bitter drink. I cried out from the intensity of the pain as Miriam began to clean my feet with water, and then applied a thick paste to the area of the bite. I felt a blur of vision, and a cold sweat began to wash over all parts of my body from the feverish temperature that spiked in my body. I managed to see Asaf enter the tent in a panic, sit down next to me and begin to pray quietly, calling on Archangel Raphael for healing and Archangel Michael for protection and salvation. Asaf repeated the prayer several times until I began to hear his voice getting weaker, my consciousness dissolved, despite the pain in my legs that bothered me and came in throbbing beats at a fast pace. I lost consciousness and began to dream. In my dream I was sitting inside a deep cave in the village with my legs crossed facing the light outside.

A large viper entered the cave, crawling in a slow, coiled movement like a spring, raised its head and stared at me. His split pink tongue protruded from his mouth as he uttered an eerie hiss. I look at his brown skin and the shapes scattered on it, his scales glittering and his black eyes mesmerizing and opaque. The snake looked straight into my eyes and started talking to me. "I am the snake that bit you, Nimrod. I gave you a taste of my venom when I stung your right leg. My venom has the power to help your transformation, raise your life force and create an eternal change within you. If you agree to accept my venom and allow it to dissolve in your body, you will be able to free yourself from the darkness in you. You will also be able to shed fears and negative influences in your life."

The snake began to demonstrate his words by shedding his skin, while moving in circles, his eyes hooded and mind in a trance. When the snake was left bare, I saw the entirety of the shed skin resting on the floor of the cave, shredded. "I am your power animal, symbolizing your complex soul. I ask you today to stay with me without going back to your past, where you felt neglect and lack of self-love. Because what was is already over. Resisting my venom and the transformation you can go through will cause you more suffering, unnecessary pain and danger to your life. Move forward like the snake, slowly and quietly into the future. Learn from me to be modest, be careful not to hurt people or yourself; you have been warned..." he said and disappeared.

When I opened my eyes again, after three days of being unconscious, I noticed Miriam and Asaf sitting next to me. It became clear to me that they had not left my side for a moment the entire time... Miriam was smiling at me, and she said, "Welcome back, cousin."

My two cousins, my friends, Asaf and Miriam, were sitting close to me, watching... Asaf said that they have been with me for days and nights, praying, chanting, applying healing ointments and hydrating me with herbal tea. I thanked Miriam and Asaf sincerely for their dedication and for bringing me back to life from that near-death experience. Overcome with excitement, Asaf sang to me our childhood song:

"To the place we go and from which we run,

We will rise up and ascend to the One..."

Miriam approached me and again, to my dismay, made me sip bitter tea from the branches of sharp varthemia and white broom and explained that they had the power to neutralize the snake's venom in my body and heal me for good. Later Asa entered the tent smiling, happy that I had regained consciousness. "You have gained friends who truly love you, you are a real family, the family of the soul. In a few days, you will be able to get up on your feet and go about your business, young man. I wish that the virtue of the powerful viper snake will lead your life to renewal, creativity, and wisdom. Now, perhaps, you have awakened to other possibilities, so take responsibility and create the reality of abundance in your life."

Asaf

Chapter 1

Early in the morning, I joyfully show up at my teacher Asa's tent at the edge of the camp for another spiritual lesson. A month has already passed since our confirmation ceremony. Nimrod returned to function fully, and I felt that we were taking another spiritual step in studying and applying the knowledge we gained to benefit the Unity Congregation.

Asa welcomed me warmly and led me to sit in the shade of the palm trees, a spot that is a lush, peaceful oasis. He said, "The sun is the source of life and light, it is the driving force of life in the universe and creation. Its light is the knowledge with which we are united through the merging of consciousness. Now I ask you to sit on the ground and straighten your back!" Since I was already sitting on a cushion on the ground, I immediately straightened my back and prepared for his next instructions. When he saw that I did as he said, he continued to explain, "By sitting this way on the ground, you absorb its forces, and counter the forces of the sky and the sun that come from a center of light above your head. The life forces in the universe reach above your head, pass through the top of your head, slightly above it, to a point known as the 'crown,' and then descend through the spine down your back to the bottom of your feet, through the base of your spine.

Since time immemorial, healers have known how to channel the solar forces to elevate the soul, to move by chariot or their aura cloaks of light to other spaces in the universe."

He began to teach me how to build the envelope of the cloak of light around my body and apply it, then added, "You will learn to ride through the cloak of your light to the home planet from which your soul came to planet Earth and draw power and life forces from there. I will guide you to reach Sirius, which is the twin sun of our sun, and the stars of the Pleiades guided by their Sirian teachers, in the center of the galaxy. I will connect you to the secrets of the Ark of the Covenant, hidden in one of the caves of Qumran safeguarded by the Unity Congregation. In about twelve years from now, you will take my place and succeed me. You will be the guardian of the Ark of the Covenant at the energy gate of Qumran. Sirius, which is located at the center of our galaxy, is connected to an ancient library of knowledge linked to the records of knowledge on this planet, through ancient codes. Many beings of light and spiritual healers come from the area of Sirius and the stars of the Pleiades, known also as the 'Seven Sisters.' Earth is the eighth sister of the Pleiades and is seeded with knowledge and life from this source. The developing planet Earth is intended to serve and empower the Creator and the eighth field of knowledge, which in a spiral movement strengthens the connection to the Pleiades and fertilizes the entire galaxy with an endless dance of light. Planet Earth is destined to later become a school of love, similar to advanced stars, such as Venus and Sirius, which are a forward field of light in creation, which exists, similar to the model found in the temple of love, in the stars moving up the steps of light. The cosmic school of light and love is intended to enable everyone in the universe rapid consciousness transformation and a complete ascension, out of complete balance and healing in their being."

I closed my eyes as my teacher told me to, and I felt him touch me lightly on the shoulder and on the top of my head. He began to delegate to my body a light of warmth and love, and I began to see a vision in which I quickly moved to another light sphere. In my vision, a huge white owl with golden eyes came and sat beneath me. He lifted me on his back flying towards the center of the galaxy. This wonderful owl finally landed on the blue star Sirius and dropped me at the entrance of a beautiful golden temple, shining with a strong and blinding light. I then heard my teacher Asa asking me to enter through for a 'Heart Initiation' which unites the living bodies in the mantle of light and transforms them into a multigalactic consciousness. This gives me a powerful, clear, and stable spiritual core. It is an intensity that gives strength and balance, through which I will be able to dedicate myself by creation to serve with love and purity, as a spiritual messenger of God. When the powerful ordeal ended, I retired to rest, flooded with new experiences and full of admiration. I rested and waited for Nimrod in the cave before we joined the rest of the community for evening studies. I was filled with satisfaction and felt more connected than ever before to the Unity Congregation and my mission within it.

Chapter 2

After resting from the day's labor and dinner, Nimrod and I headed to the meeting at the Library of Knowledge. About twenty members sat waiting quietly in the cave that was dotted with large wax candles that spread light and a subtle fragrance of honey. We joined the other men who sat in a semi-circle with their faces turned to Judah, the elder of the council, who spoke to the knowledge-thirsty listeners patiently waiting. Judah began to talk about angels, as a continuation of something that had previously been discussed.

"On the first day of creation, the angels and the spiritual powers were formed. This happened in seven stages, when the angels were God's chosen not to fail in sin, and their holiness was confirmed and eternally validated by God," Judah explained. "After God created the angels, he put them to the test, to see if they would obey him or betray his word. The devil, known as 'Lucifer' or 'the bearer of light,' was the highest-ranking angel and the closest to God, in charge of the cherubs. After them in the hierarchy came the Seraphim, and below them the angels. The Archangel is the youngest son of God, Archangel Michael. He is the lord of all the angels who report to him. He also protects and saves from Satan. A third of the angles created by God chose to follow the devil who lost his consciousness, rebelled against God, and wanted to be even more superior than him. He 'fell from heaven' or the higher spiritual worlds and became demons and unclean spirits. Two-thirds of the angels, that is, the vast majority, chose not to follow Satan, and the holiness of their souls was confirmed and validated for good. They are the chosen angels, 'the chosen ones,' also known as the 'holy angels,' as opposed to the sullied angels. The holy angels are the Irim, among them the 'guardians,' watchful observers, who ensure that God's will is fulfilled. All the angels were created at the same time, and their number will not increase. They exist forever and cannot be destroyed. The angels were all created holy at first but were given the option to choose the opposite. Some chose to become demons, and some were given eternal purity and could no longer choose to sin. They were stripped of the power to choose to sin or opposition.

"Their status is higher than that of man, but lower than that of the Messiah. They appear to be genderless and have immortal strength and power. The body of angels consists of a spiritual body, and they have emotion and will, but their knowledge is less than that of God and they are not omniscient like Him. Gabriel is an angel whose name means 'Champion of God,' a judge of what is happening on earth and the harbinger of divine revelations. The 'Seraphim' are angelic beings with six wings, who are close to God and praise Him constantly. They cleanse by fire, and their faces are of a lion, a calf, a man, and an eagle. The Cherubs are the highest in the hierarchy of heavenly beings. They have two wings; they are luminous, and they are swift to move.

'Satan' is called 'cherub' and was formerly the head of the cherubs, while Archangel Michael, as mentioned, headed the angels. Satan is at the base of his creation in a higher category than Michael. Angels have many roles. They praise, bow, and faithfully carry out the will of God, who protects and saves, but also executes judgment, as in the biblical story of the destruction of the cities 'Sodom and Gomorrah,' and like the tenth plague in Egypt, before the Exodus of the Israelites. The law of Moses was also given through the mediation of the angels. They prophesize, warn, guide their believers to the truth in action, and answer their prayers. They encourage the soul and help in the process of spiritual ascension and protect communities." Judah concluded the lesson for the evening and some of the students left the cave. Those who left went to rest and sleep for the night. Some of us stayed to study Torah in shifts throughout the night. Nimrod went to sleep for a few hours and prepared to return to the group in the early hours of the morning.

Chapter 3

On our way to a pre-breakfast dip in the mikveh, Nimrod, myself, and many Qumran locals step quietly, slowly trailing along the paths toward our shared destination. All community members abide by the rules, remain quiet, rarely speak, and stay attentive. I start talking to Nimrod, but he does not listen to me and cuts me off like a spear, like someone possessed by a demon. I try to bring up the topic of "freedom of choice" for discussion between us, as we approach the water, but his tone only increases, like the sound of a massive waterfall. "True freedom," he says, "is a situation in which a person puts himself as an individual before his fellow man and before God. How else can we accomplish something in this world and in our lives without first trying to realize our personal path as a priority?" While he speaks, I notice senior council members coming and standing next to us, including Judah, the head of the Council of Sages of Unity Congregation. I try to get Nimrod to quiet down by touching his shoulder, but to no avail. I want to tell him to refrain from saying things that may put him in danger. But Nimrod, almost possessed, ignores my attempts. He continues with full vigor to speak on the same subject, tries to accentuate his words and even voices further thoughts to prove his points.

Judah hears Nimrod and in an untypical manner, decides to directly intervene, taking a step forward and stands in front of us. A black cloud approaches my heart, telling me that something very unpleasant is about to happen. I touch Nimrod's arm and jerk it several times, to try once again to draw his attention to what is happening, to the danger he is facing, alas my attempt is futile.

Judah turns his words to Nimrod and says, "Nimrod, why are you so boisterous, breaking the Unity Congregation's rules of silence? Is there a reason for your mental turmoil?"

Nimrod's cheeks turn slightly red when he points his gaze to Judah, and his cheeky eyes meet Judah's face. Nimrod turns to him and continues, "Are the rules of the Unity cult justified and higher than the truth of the individual? Is personal freedom an issue that can be abolished for the sake of the common good in the name of God's will? Or can the importance of this value be reduced, blinding the eyes of the people living in this cult, claiming that God's will is the only will? Isn't this a foolish thought? You are harming people. This is damaging them in the name of God!"

Judah was filled with rage and restrainedly replied to Nimrod with a stiff upper lip, "Do you not think that God is greater than any simplistic definition, you included? Do not go about taking his name in vain, as you pretend to understand through a simplistic and selfish perception that narrows his magnitude and place in the universe and in the life of the individual."

Nimrod hastened to answer him with a shout, "How

do you not see the injustice you are causing people, when you try to deny them personal freedom in its most fundamental and simplest form?"

"Hush, my son," said Judah. "You probably cannot understand how things settle and unite with each other in an exemplary divine order. You must wait patiently and learn more, to increase your wisdom and knowledge to master this question."

My heart began to pound strongly, and the dark cloud that I felt began to get even closer, spreading within me. I experienced palpable danger as the cloud began to envelop me in an even more physical way, while Nimrod continued to talk more and even began to curse. "Damn you, you son of a bitch, God will take you away," Nimrod continued to curse Judah with insults, despite Judah's earlier request of him to be quiet. Judah then turned to one of the council members by his side, and with a silent nod, gave him a signal to intervene and stop Nimrod's speech. Two council members began to advance towards Nimrod. They grabbed him from both his sides and led him to a place of confinement in a room at the end of Qumran. They locked him up there for a day until the twelve council members tried him. He was in breach of the rules we undertook to obey in the confirmation ceremony. We both knew that condemning or cursing a senior member of the council in public or taking God's name in vain would be considered an egregious violation of a sacred oath.

I was overcome with sadness and sorrow for Nimrod, who once again in his life was facing real life-threatening danger. This time, unlike back when we were children, I cannot simply run away to save my soul. Our lives are so deeply connected – I cannot escape. I have no choice now but to go through the necessary path, without the ability to prevent the looming, harsh fate.

I turn my gaze forward and see John talking to old Judah, and I realize that he was the informant. John must have told him about Nimrod's plans to gather the youth of the tribe. Judah will now think that Nimrod is planning a defiant act of rebellion against the community. My teacher Menachem approaches, and Judah probably shares with him what John told him a moment ago. I leave Nimrod and go to the edge of Qumran, climb the mountain, and begin to pray. I ask God to spare Nimrod from punishment or ruin. I beg the Creator and cry out to the heavens, hoping with all of my heart that an easy solution will be found. Wishing with all of me that Nimrod be saved from the death penalty pursuant to the laws of the Unity Congregation.

Chapter 4

"Let me go!" I heard Nimrod scream. "Damned may you be!" He cursed one of the two men who held him from both sides and prevented him from going wild or escaping. His hands were tied with a rope behind his back and his clothes, which he had not changed for a day, were stained. His black hair was disheveled, his eyes were red with rage and sorrow, and his gaze was directed downwards at the ground.

As members of the congregation began to gather in front of the cave, I looked at Nimrod from afar and my heart was torn to shreds inside me. About fifty people gathered, as spectators and witnesses to the verdict, whereby Nimrod would be stoned to death in the cave. The council of the twelve arrived at the spot, among them old Judah. They entered the slightly dark cave first, which turned out to be deeper on the inside than it looked on the outside. Judah stepped in first, and the other council members followed him in as a group. In the center of the cave gaped a pit, into which they were going to put Nimrod. Next to the pit awaited a large mound of stones that had been collected and set there in advance. Nimrod and the two men, the angels of death watching him, now entered the cave, and after them we all began to form a circle, followed by more people forming outer circles.

The women were not allowed to participate in the execution. They were ordered to stay in the camp far from the scene. I stood in the second peripheral circle, crowded, and wrapped in the sense of belonging to peers who believe that justice and truth are being served. I was disconnected from my emotions. The sorrow in my heart began to blur and was replaced by a cold sweat. The prickly air closed in on me, until I felt a kind of paralysis in my body. Nimrod was pushed into the pit, and his face now carried the expression of great regret. He whined and cried, said he was sorry and asked for forgiveness from old Judah, for breaking the rules he only recently swore to keep. Judah's face, however, was completely cold as he ordered the commencement of the ceremony with a slight head gesture, after which the members of the council began to collect stones from the pile and hold them in their hands. The other members followed suit, holding the death stones in their hands. With my feet planted like a tree gripped with terror, I did not move, completely breathless. I continued to watch the unfolding spectacle, frozen, unable to move. I felt that my soul had left my body. I kept closing and opening my eyes as the stoning process began.

Stones were thrown like a shower of brimstone on Nimrod's body, and his loud cries slowly weakened, as if he had finally accepted his death, defeated in silent acquiescence. His spirit was as if broken in two and cut to pieces. Everything happened in perfect silence. The "hive" operated in unison. The members of the community acted in exemplary unity. An hour later, it was over. I looked quickly at Nimrod lying on the ground of the killing pit, with his face turned towards the ground, and his body covered with stones. His shirt and head looked bloodied, his dark hair had turned red, and there was no trace of the uprightness of his bold frame. I left the cave with the crowd, holding back the tears that were waiting to break out, frozen.

When I came out of the darkness of the cave into the light, I saw Miriam by the palm tree looking into the distance and waiting for me, worried. I stepped towards her, floating, my feet barely touching the hard soil. I reached her, finally collapsing into her embrace, letting out a cry. I bawled for the loss of my friend. I clearly knew in my heart that I had to withdraw from the cult and leave. "Miriam," I whispered sobbing as my dream was shattered and with it a light, which is now far from here and from me.

"I do not know how to move on from here. I have lost all faith in God," said Miriam. "The time has come for us to go and create a new dream. We will leave for Mount Tabor, return to your home, and create our lives there. We will dream up a new dream together."

We walked slowly down the path, holding each other. We moved away from Nimrod's stoning site and we both noticed the skin of the snake that had been shed this morning on the bright and dusty soil of Qumran.

Miriam

Chapter 1

This morning, I went out in search of Asa as I could hardly get any sleep last night. I was devastated over Nimrod's death. Mourning my cousin's passing, I sought Asa's advice and relief for my pain. Asa greeted me at the entrance to his tent with tired eyes, evidence of his own lack of sleep last night.

When he saw my condition, he rushed to support me with both his hands and allowed me to lean on him so as not to fall. He tried to comfort me as I sobbed, and once I finally did, he offered to help me with another visit to the cleansing cave for a chance to revisit another memory of my past life. He said that it would be a way to let go of an old pain that keeps coming back, though its origin is from another life. It could offer some insight into my present life and the incident with Nimrod.

We walked together slowly to the cave. Asa lit a little fire, heated a vessel with water and added vegetable oil, myrrh, and frankincense from a small clay bottle, which he brought in the bag made of woven palm branches he had carried. I lay down on a sheep's wool rug and began to breathe circularly, letting go, into the heart, sensing the soothing aromatic oils. I quickly returned to the memory of my life as a Hebrew in Egypt and stepped again with bare feet on the cool marble floor of the hallowed halls at Tel El Amarna, the kingdom of my grandfather, King Akhenaten. My vision changed. I moved on the time continuum several years forward in my life as Isis teaching the class of the twelve priesthood acolytes. I saw her lying on the floor crying bitterly. Isis held the body of her dead student in a desperate hug, hoping it would bring him back to life. She looked at his pale, lifeless face, and was overcome with guilt. She felt that he died because of a mistake she made and her incorrect decision to confirm him too early in the process, unprepared for his undertaking. She realized that she misjudged the situation and was now experiencing the consequence. Her mind was confused and tormented, and she felt a burning loss at his death, trapped in despair. The air she breathed began to escape her lungs and her eyes became two small cracks, like skylights, through which the world was reflected to her in a narrow, slanted image. She asked to die instead of her student and saw no point or possibility of living without him. His cold body, wet from her tears reminded her that she would not find him in his body, even if she asked as his soul had already moved away... Finally, she slowly loosened her grip, placed his body on the floor, and started walking out to return to her residence where she may find comfort or talk to someone close and to mourn her loss.

***

The image of the vision in Miriam's mind changed and moved several days forward in the sequence of time. Isis is now in a boat, which is being rowed by two of Pharaoh's servants across the Nile. They took her to an island far away from Tel El Amarna, Akhenaten's kingdom, so she could observe and recover from the crisis she was going through following the death of her beloved student. Isis lay exhausted, peering out of the sides of the ship moving in slow motion at a constant rowing pace. Looking through the straw slits in the shadowed boat, she notices the giant Sphinx slowly revealing its face to her from a distance. Without neither words nor sounds, the sphinx asked, "Who are you? Do you know yourself? What is the virtue in your life actions?"

His questions remain unanswered. Her strength is running out, her head is dizzy, and she is on the verge of fainting. Losing track of time... How many hours have passed? Has it been days? months? She shifts between wakefulness and sleep, to a dark place devoid of light to which her soul sails without control or will. Then one of Pharaoh's servants pours drinking water into her mouth from a long, brown waterskin. Pharaoh's servants allow her to fast, for they know that the high priests have the power to perform all kinds of mysterious acts. Therefore, they fulfill teacher Ankh-Aton's instructions regarding her treatment with uncompromising obedience. Finally, after quite a while, the boat stops. They help her out carefully and bring her to the depths of a small village on the island.

They place her gently in a wooden hut with a thatched roof in the shade of the trees, and quickly return to the boat, rushing as they came, back to the white halls of the Egyptian kingdom. Now Isis will be able to isolate herself and observe everything that happened, ask for peace and calm in her life. She asks, "How can I observe, faded and lost, separated from my powers and away from all? Will I ever return to my life in Egypt's white temple halls? My heart is broken. Will I be able to teach and serve the divine once again?" The crisis is deep, her being is falling apart. "If only I could be used in some way as a servant of some sort," she muses with a sense of guilt and exhaustion, clinging to the last of her strength. "The taste of failure constantly burns my heart. I made a mistake; how can I make my atonement?" These thoughts echo in her mind repeatedly. "My beloved student paid with his life; will I ever atone for the disaster that happened? Perhaps this is the right time for me to leave life on earth and return my soul to my Creator"? Suicidal thoughts of despair run through her mind, and she begs to die. Dark thoughts cloud her mind, as she feels that strange faces begin to surround her from all sides. She hears voices, a foreign language ringing, followed by dark eyes.

They curiously glare at her body, which lies limp and lifeless on the surface of the hard ground. As she disappears into a valley of existence far, far away, she realizes that the strange, dark, foreign faces staring at her from all sides are the worried islanders. They gathered curiously to watch a strange "gift from heaven" that they just received. They know that Isis did not come to them for no reason. They look at the fair, small-framed goddess, her thin body, spread out like a withered and lifeless plant on their soil. The sages of the tribe informed them of this many years ago; that a day would come, and the daughter of the White Eagle would come to their home, announcing the coming of love and peace to the island. As she closes her eyes and drifts off to sleep, to the upper dimensions, she catches a glimpse of them forming a circle of prayer and healing around her, singing a song of praise to their wise ancestors, who are in the upper worlds. Now she knows what she did not for quite a while, able to let go of the pain. She loses consciousness. Golden rays of light reach a spiral structure that appears as a glowing vortex to pick her up. From inside of it, entities of the tribal forefathers, come out with their plowed faces radiating rays of wisdom. They come to her wearing white tunics, their hair is long and adorned with bright feathers, their eyes soft and full of compassion. They dance in a circle of joy and thanksgiving, merging into her like a circle of stars, filling her with unity and warmth. One of them reaches out his hand and leads her confidently through the wonderous tunnel, knowing the way to where she wants to be. There is no more sorrow, only peace saturated with sweetness and gentleness, and the path looks familiar. She has returned to where she belongs.

In the distance she sees her father and mother waiting, accompanying her as if they never left her side. At some distance behind them, Osiris, her dead student reclusive and hesitant. Endless joy, love, and longing for each other. "Osiris," she says softly, "Are you, in all your beauty and strength alive, my dear student"? My memory as Isis takes me back to the great white halls. I am trying to understand how it all happened. I am trying to hold on to some thread of understanding about the results of my actions, and the memory of the disaster is starting to come back to me.

Today she turned forty, wearing a white dress adorned with gold fringes, black braids coming down from her head decked with a gold jewel in the shape of a snake that reaches the center of her forehead, carrying the engraved symbol of the sun. In her hand is a crystal ball scepter symbolizing the sacred teachers' service of the divine. Isis looks at Osiris, the beloved student, and thinks, how many years have passed since he began his studies and grew into a sturdy and handsome young man. (As Miriam, I recognize Osiris as Nimrod, who is with me in this life with the Essenes). His brightness illuminates the great space as his fellow students pale in comparison. She taught them all, and over the years they became well versed in all the eternal laws and the high truths of God. Despite their great beauty and spiritual height, in their hearts a special and rare spot of light is reserved for Osiris. All in the hall of the sacred pool in preparation for the confirmation in the water. Everyone knows the extent of the grave responsibility and the consequences confirmation will have on their lives, or so it seems to her at this glorious hour, when the white marble walls envelop them in their soft bright light. Nefritini, one of Isis' students, looks at her with unquestionable admiration, and she returns a loving smile as if to a cherished daughter.

"Osiris is going to be one of the greatest teachers in the temples, if not the best," she muses, and her heart fills with pleasure and satisfaction. "Soon he will become a priest, and he will serve with me in the great pyramid. He is powerful, and at the same time there is a flicker of brazen power that clouds the perfection of his radiant aura." Though she represses these thoughts, as they are pointless after all, are they not? I wonder what attracts her to him and why she secretly prefers him over the other students? Is it the healing powers within him to which she is drawn? Indeed, in her soul she expects that he will be a special part of her team of servants of the light. Now she immerses the students in the clear pool and is elated with joy she has never before experienced. Like shining gems, her students flock, and it seems that after this spiritual baptism they move to new realms from which there is no way back. In unison, their aura shines, and their faces radiate endless peace, which illustrates the unmediated connection and the alliance they have just made with their Creator. Osiris' beauty spectacularly shines as he emerges from the pool of water as a lion with a fiery red mane, so beautiful and so powerful. Isis notices the all-consuming desire, pride and power that drives Osiris to demand even higher supremacy. Addiction to power. A deep concern for his well-being begins to resonate, and for the first time since meeting him, she admits to herself that something has gone wrong in their lives, and that this is an ominous sign.

***

Once again, the image returns in which Miriam sees Isis lying on the island ground, and the members of the tribe circle around her. Isis notices that her soul is far away, in the dimension of Osiris, free of care or pain in levitation, without a physical body. Isis is taken away by a mysterious gravity to a white hall that stands high in a blue sky, garlanded with fluffy white clouds. "This is not the time for answers about Osiris," she hears a deep and powerful voice speaking to her in her mind. "You must know the eternity of the soul of Osiris in every encounter in further incarnations expected on your path." Isis again in the White Hall in the heavens, levitating across a long and bright corridor, passing rooms on its sides. Her consciousness is directed to her destination independently, as if walking in a familiar place to which she returned many times when her life had ended. It is at the entrance of a large and spacious hall, in the center of which stands a royal chair prettified with pure gold embellishments radiating far and wide around it. On the chair sits the primordial Creator in the form of a large golden egg of indescribable light. Like a magic wand, she feels drawn to this source of light, to find shelter in its love that heals and unites the truth of her being. The power began to speak in her consciousness in a warm and loving, soothing and caressing voice, "You are standing in the hall of halls in the abode of the Creator, but everything your eyes see is adjusted to the convenience of your perception, from patterns and concepts known to you from your life. Different souls see me, the Creator, in different ways shaped by their beliefs and culture. I am the primordial Creator. The Creator of everything, in everything; uniting everything. I am the unity of all the forces that exist in creation. Love is the core of me, the supreme and central force that gives the universe momentum to grow and develop. Love returns you to the source from which you parted, and to which you return more enlightened and radiant at the end of your life's journey. Love is the force that unifies your return home to the core of the self, which is waiting to be fulfilled along with its ultimate purpose. Love moves us to the rousing, beneficent whole.

"Cosmic growth, moving in a spiral motion, allows love to be revealed through infinite experiences. Remember, love has a purpose: to reveal itself in every viable way in the universe before returning to the divine source, to expand its boundaries, to reverberate in one's being, forever. Knowing yourself in love and knowing the God who dwells in you are your one goal."

The ovoid source of power began to change its form on the golden chair and became a mammoth diamond radiating rays of gold and light. He continued his words and said, "Knowing one's complete and full self in all its aspects is likened to an enormous diamond, revealing its prongs and introducing new layers and new degrees of depth each time. This exposure is the work of alchemy, in which you experience in your life illumination and then you fulfill a purpose designed by divine forces in creation.

"Through understanding your heart, you will discover the meaning of unconditional love, the source of the movement of the development of creation. Refine your heart, so you can live in balance and harmony without causing destruction. Looking inward and paying attention to your heart will lead to knowledge that will be heard in the depths of your being, its wisdom and love, for your utmost good! Your own self is a smart instrument that has the power to direct you to the path of your spiritual needs and goals. It is right for you to use the tools that I encrypted for you in the depths of your being, tools that are meant to illuminate the way back to the place from which you came, the womb of creation. Your ascension and self-maturation are achieved through your inner power and opening your heart to the spiritual reality that surrounds you. The voice of the self is the voice of the soul, which is heard in pure silence.

"The aspiration to harmonize your resolve with the divine will and its fulfillment will give you eternal achievements, and you will accumulate them during many lives, one after another, until you reach the ultimate goal: the return home to the perfection of your pure being, where you will merge in perfection and unity with your Creator."

Silence prevailed in the white hall as the force concluded its speech. "Come closer to me now," the force tells me. With apprehension, I slowly take a few steps towards the powerful, radiant light. I felt the light collecting me and embracing me into infinite arms. "Now look again and remember what happened in your life that left you in such agony," The force asked of me with an encouraging gentleness. "Look within to be able to contain, to release your pain, and to heal your heart."

My memories returned to the white halls and to the house where we lived in Tel El Amarna. As Isis walks through the halls, she meets Horus coming towards her, and his face portends grave concern. We hug and greet each other with peace and love, which charges us both with strength and light. "Osiris walks crooked paths," Horus says. "Many priests saw him in the company of the priests of Amon, the enemies of our teacher and our king, from whom he warned us many times. He is insatiably seeking the advice of others and the way to return to the power that he experienced during his confirmation. He is looking for a shortcut to power, after losing the balance of purity in his physical body.

"Isis, you must make haste and help him. Keep him away and warn him of the looming danger. He is searching for the dark devices in the Amon-priestly rituals. There are people who have heard that he connects his body to the black tourmaline stone generator, which we were warned about by our teacher Ankh-Aton. Osiris is restless and ready to fulfill his desire in any possible way and at any cost." Isis parts with Horus and rushes through the many corridors looking for her teacher, Ankh-Aton, to ask him for guidance. She finds him sitting alone in his room, glimmering with serenity.

"I waited for you, my dear child. But you have come late. What is done cannot be undone, this is the way your soul chose to learn unconditional love," he says in his mysterious and loving way. She does not quite understand his words, but her heart tells her there is unwelcome news behind them. Pain begins to seep into her soul, followed by panic and fear. Isis says goodbye to her dear teacher and continues on her way to search for the whereabouts of her student Osiris. Passing through dark corridors, she makes her way to temple of the priests of Amon. Outside the halls, she meets the bright sun in the center of the sky, passing between the kingdom's well-kept trees, the white water fountains placed in perfect symmetry along the boulevard. The king's chariot awaits to quickly take her to the waiting royal wooden boat. Finally, after a long voyage, Isis arrives at a large city, where she walks through broad streets, guided by the power of love, which drives her to the whereabouts of Osiris in an ornate and ostentatious temple of the priests of Amun. Foreign, dark, and unfamiliar faces pass by her. Priests wearing black robes with attached bonnets hooding their heads. Her heart shrinks with dark thoughts. The surroundings are obviously charged with intrigues and conspiracies. She hears the thoughts of dark priests who want to take power for themselves and overthrow king Akhenaten from his noble throne. These formations of thought and emotion arouse deep disgust in her heart and make her feel nauseous and dizzy. Fear for the fate of Osiris intensifies as she takes slow steps. Her legs betray her, as if they were reluctant to carry her to his location.

Finally, she reaches the main sanctuary, where, on a large, raised platform she sees a black tourmaline stone generator directed towards a ceiling with a broad opening facing the sky. Until that moment, she had never seen a device like it, but she knew a lot about the dangers lying in wait should it ever be used. It affects the core energy and directs energy from it to the center of the earth and from the earth to the physical body. Priests use it sparingly, to heighten vitality. Unlike them, the priests of light use the clear and white crystals out of awareness and out of pure spiritual goals. A priest who has not overcome negative energies and whose intentions are not pure, it is better not to use black tourmaline, as it will make one feel a chain of unpleasant and even traumatic events, putting their life at risk.

Her eyes began to scour the room, anxiously looking for Osiris, and here in a dark side corner she sees a body slumped over, limply on top of one of the dark devices in the hall. She kneels at his feet and tries to turn him over to find out his identity. His body is still warm, as if he saved his last breath for her. But his sweet soul left his body a long time ago and took off to other and distant realms. "Osiris," cries Isis and embraces his body. She bursts into tears out of the depths of her soul, tries in vain to grasp what is left of him, refusing to accept their forced premature separation.

After a long journey, which seemed even longer to her this time, she returned to Tel El Amarna. Exhausted and with slow steps, she enters the white halls and commands one of Pharaoh's servants to return to the scene of the tragedy, remove Osiris' body and prepare it for proper burial in the white temple. She continues from there to the abode of teacher Ankh-Aton, to find comfort and healing for her aching heart. He waits for her with a compassionate look on his face. "I have been waiting for you, my child," he says briefly and pulls her closer to him. All the dams of her emotions opened releasing a cry like never before. He lets her go, and when she finally calms down, he orders her to sit on a chair by his side. She takes a deep breath, searches in vain for the right words and asks, "What did I do wrong, and what am I to learn from this?" He answers her with silence and wraps her with love. The water test, which Osiris did not successfully pass, which you as his teacher failed to properly train him for, is intended to prove that the student has the power to move in the upper worlds freely, safely, and faithfully. A student must carry out all actions without leaning on any external factors. As a result of the experience in the water confirmation ritual and the knowledge one acquires in the higher worlds, one can develop this ability and create changes in the higher realm of their being. However, if something from their personal preferences or their narrow personal will interfere, consequences will be different.

The student will lose the purpose of their action and will experience obscurity and confusion on their path. The water test is designed to teach self-control and to develop the ability to listen faithfully to lofty principles and ideals, despite personal tendencies that try to sway one to other directions. A student must know how to rely on correct diagnosis and sound and stable judgment. To rely on the truth regarding the reality of their life, with a willingness to immediately abandon any idea, illusion, or tendency that hinders them from the ultimate path that furthers them to the love of God and the truth.

"Osiris failed to develop these inner qualities at a high level. He wanted to recover his supreme feelings, which he experienced in his encounter with the upper worlds in an external way to his being, as a means of escaping from the physical world. He did not behave as a balanced diagnostician of the divine power that lies within him, as a priest who knows that he must strengthen and preserve power out of a life of modesty, moderation, and a balanced path, in order to fulfill goals and implement values on earth.

"You, dear Isis, did not know how to recognize those very weaknesses, since you favored him over your other students. You did not have your spiritual sight as a diagnostic tool and correct judgment of the facts of your lives. You have allowed the inclination of your own heart to keep you away from the ultimate path, and therefore you did not properly prepare him for the water test. Your walk along the spiritual paths is meant for you to learn unconditional love and to rise above your narrow personal desires, to act out of a spiritual truth, which corresponds with God's will. Now stop what you have been doing and engage in a deep observation of everything that happened, until you receive a higher call to return to the kingdom, clean and empowered."

Isis now realized that force understands her with full compassion and forgives her completely, and he even asks her to continue on her path and grow from the mistake she made. He supports everything that happens to her as part of their mutual journey of growth and learning. He wishes for her to discover unconditional love through further experiences, and for that she must return to her body and her life on earth.

It has now become clear to her that she had been given a priceless gift. The gift of life and flesh. Inside the body it is possible to experience life on earth in a tangible and creative way. Some of us will even give birth to other souls from our wombs. Our body gives us a feeling of love and joy; it takes us to other places and offers us a way to learn and develop that are not possible in any other way, but still our being is not our body but much more than that.

Living in our bodies leads to complete awareness of the true nature of reality and how the universe works. Life is love and pain, growth, and joy. Life is a set of lessons chosen by the soul in the world above, lessons the essence of which is love and relationships. This is the main goal of the study of life on earth. This is the reason why souls are fulfilled in familial groups, each of which accept their roles in each other's lives, for the purpose of experiencing and learning together. We live and die in groups of loving souls. We leave the earth and experience the world of difficulties again as groups. Souls returning together repeatedly. At the time of death, the soul leaves the physical body and embarks on a journey whose goals are rest, learning and further healing, as well as reunification with their loved ones who have died in the past. In every transition of life, we are given the opportunity to work and strive towards our utmost good and the perfection of all parts of the self in us.

The purpose of life is to experience every aspect of being in a body on earth, but a soul is a part of God, and is whole and good. When we return to the upper worlds, we rejoin together and enjoy the peace of union with all our loved ones who have departed from the world before us. The unity of all life occurs when we learn about mercy and compassion. This is the universal love for every living being, and this is learned from life experiences in all their complexities and perspectives. I returned to my body from the journey of spiritual recollection, as Miriam living with the Essenes, and my head is dizzy and a little heavy. The ground I was lying on was a little hard, yet in my heart I felt new mental powers that I had not imagined existed before in my life. The recollections of my transition as Isis of Egypt gave them to me. I remembered that I was Nimrod's spiritual teacher and experienced his death there in Egypt as well, and I understood the source of the pain I still feel today. I said goodbye to my teacher Asa and went to look for Asaf to share my experiences with him.

The next morning, Asaf and I decided to leave the Essenes, to return to the village at the foot of Mount Tabor, where his parents were and where he grew up most of his life. I wanted to say goodbye to my brother John, who decided to stay in the cult despite the departure of Asaf and me. I knew that he remained in the trusted hands of the community members, who would continue to take care of him and all his needs, educate him and shape his life according to his skills and abilities. Qumran was now his family, and he felt part of the Unity Congregation. I wanted to move away together with my beloved Asaf from the ruins of the terrible rupture we experienced and start a new life somewhere else. I told Asaf, after the reminiscence session at the passage of other lives, that I was going to part with my brother. "I'm also going to say goodbye to the only one who remains significant to me in the Unity Congregation, my teacher Asa. I need his guidance to get new direction for my life, and to know how to continue from here on." I watched as his legs barely carried him along the dirt paths leading to Asa's tent, but he walked resolutely to the radiant tent at the edge of Qumran.

Asaf

Chapter 1

Asa was sitting with his legs crossed on a round cushion when I came to seek his help. He was sitting somber at the entrance to his tent. "I've been waiting for you," he said, "and I even transmitted a thought to you in the spiritual sphere, in which I asked you to come to me before you and Miriam leave us."

I was dumbfounded. How did he know our plan even before I shared it with him? But I remembered that he was endowed with such a broad spiritual vision and that he could see inner things related to souls so close to him, like me and like Miriam. He looked at me with his black, dark, piercing eyes, leaned towards me and asked me to sit on a cushion next to him. My words were lost, and a wave of sadness enveloped me. Tears started streaming down my cheeks and I felt lost and desperate. The events of yesterday flashed back in pieces. Images of my cousin Nimrod began to flood, threatening, hitting me with terrible anguish. I felt the ground collapse from under my feet, darkness began to fill me, and with it a dizziness that made me almost faint. Asa, who understood the very core of me, gently put his hand on my shoulder and looked at me with compassion. His gaze illuminated the darkness within me. He allowed me to experience my feelings, and now remain in the state I was in, without urging me to speak. He waited for me to calm down a bit before I spoke. After a few moments of silence, in which I gathered all my strength to speak, I told him that I did not know how I could ever get over what had happened and the loss of Nimrod.

"Asaf," he said lovingly, in his quiet voice, "it is important that you continue on your spiritual path despite the loss you are experiencing. Nimrod would also want this as your brother and as a spiritual leader who envisioned the future, that is, the right direction of humanity's growth. In a sense, even though he tried to take a shortcut in immoral and unethical behavior, he does embody a new value that will appear in the future, the value of individual freedom before freedom of a group, and only out of respect for the uniqueness of the individual person, can a society develop a more inclusive social freedom. Nimrod the Freedom Fighter would certainly want you to continue in his way, even where he failed to realize himself in the current lifetime, in the Unity Congregation. He would surely wish for you to become a teacher and spiritual leader who delivers healing to his surroundings, as you were meant to do. I think the path of a special and powerful healer is in store for you. You are designed to support the consciousness of many people and help them find God and their power within them."

I listened to his words and began to feel relief. I was encouraged and immediately found hope. That was exactly what I needed, the guidance and comfort of my beloved and very significant teacher in my life. Asa looked at me lovingly, when he saw that my strength and spirit had returned to me. "I think that you and Miriam are very suitable as partners for life, and you are soul mates. Your souls know each other because they met in a previous life transition. Even then, you loved as man and woman, intense love. However, in the reality of your previous life, you were priests who took the oath of celibacy, and therefore could not realize your love. Both of you are healers in your souls, and you are meant to restore the community in which you will live and spread light within it. You will be able to fulfill and enhance each other's power, act together to serve and help people. Together you will also heal your hearts and create a new and positive vision for a free human spirit.

"Miriam will be able to teach women through sacred dance, to lift spirits, to be a leader who conveys compassion and love in all aspects of life. She will be able to teach women to unite their souls and connect to love and truth in their hearts. She will teach them the secret of harmony in the various relationships, in the community, with their children and with their spouses.

"You are a beloved man, Asaf, and you are now being asked to go out across the country in search of the greatest teacher of our time, Jesus, son of Joseph. This teacher was born in Bethlehem and grew up in Nazareth and is a learned Jew who studied the words of the ancient sages. He created his own congregation with twelve disciples representing the twelve tribes of Israel. They are going to spread his gospel - the fulfillment of the 'Kingdom of Heaven' on earth. Jesus is today in Capernaum by the Sea of Galilee, and near your home on Mount Tabor. Jesus has many apostles. You too can be his messenger, in your own unique way, by fulfilling your own spirit on earth wholeheartedly and from a consciousness of unity."

Asa said many more things. I felt my heart skip a beat at the sound of these words. He was filled with immense excitement because he recognized the truth in the words of my teacher. Asa's words were an invitation for me to embark on a new path into the unknown, where my soul was promised salvation and ascension. I wiped the beads of sweat from my forehead, from the heat of the sun that had already risen in the open sky. I thanked Asa and said, "I will never forget you, and I know we will surely cross paths again in the future. First I must do as you say, and follow my destiny, to seek the enlightened Jesus, in order to learn from him how to develop my spirit and its virtues."

"I feel," Asa told me, "my days in the Unity Congregation are also numbered. Know that I will also leave in your wake, my student. Perhaps I will go back to Jerusalem and complete things I could not in the past. Maybe I will look for Ruth, the woman I almost married, and find out how she is doing and if she is still single like me." I thought how profound our meeting was and how transformative it must have been if Asa would also be leaving the congregation soon, following a new vision on a path connected to the depth of his soul and its unique way outside the Essene sect. He will be directly connected to the spirit of God that pulsates in him, as Jesus son of Joseph discussed with Asa in their meeting a few years ago, as the spirit of God is adapted with his new path. We parted in a warm and long embrace, which seemed to last forever in love and a new hope.

Chapter 2

It is a sweltering day. My lips are dry and thirsty for water. Every now and then, a warm breeze whisks up scents of the soil and foliage. My beloved Miriam and I sit in a circular structure on Mount Tabor, close together in the shade of the trees. Jesus son of Joseph is sitting on a rock, with Mary Magdalene on the ground by his side. Like her, we, the rest of his congregation, are sitting at his feet. Jesus suddenly stands up silent, my eyes directed at him and following his movements. He seems radiant, like a nobleman despite his modest clothing. His tunic is white, and a thin crimson cloak spills over his shoulder. His hair is a light shade of brown, flowing softly over his shoulders, his eyes are blue-gray, half shut. He is in a collected inner state of mind. Jesus places his right hand on his heart in silent prayer heard only inside his heart. From time to time his eyes open and gaze into to the crowd – a group of about fifty men and women. His flock. A wave of love washes through my heart, and an emotional tear runs down my face for no apparent reason, but the presence in his sphere of consciousness projected to us.

My mind wanders, and I am reminded again of my cousin Nimrod who was stoned to death. I am overwhelmed by sorrow. It's been a week since his death, and the pain of our separation burns inside me, coming back in waves each time I receive the love of my teacher Jesus. With that love, I am also ridden with guilt and anguish for having gained the wonder of love and a source of light, unlike Nimrod, whom I still see in a dark pit in a murky stone cave, which I left behind in the Essene sect. I think longingly of my teacher Asa, and I replay our goodbyes before leaving for my childhood home near Mount Tabor. I wonder if I will ever see Asa again sometime in the future. I recall him saying in that last meeting, "My son," and after hugging me warmly, he pressed my head against his body and said, "I know how sad you are, nothing can offer comfort. Losing a close family member is not easy. Many more days will pass before you digest your loss and your soul finds meaning and peace.

"I knew that you would leave the congregation. I understand now that you were meant to continue your life and fulfill your destiny under the guidance of a teacher, studying his messages and on a sacred vocation. Jesus teaches love and unity, and being in his company will heal your heart, as it will the hearts of many. His teachings can enlighten hearts and influence many future generations. Find him, Asaf, and tell him that Asa sent you."

My thoughts were interrupted by the sound of a woman's cry in the crowd. She knelt at Jesus' feet and sobbed, "Cure me, help me please." She continued muttering aloud indistinct words of a tormented soul. She wore earth-colored rags, and the large kerchief that wrapped her head slid down to her shoulders, leaving a small opening for her small face, which peeked out pleadingly.

Jesus placed one hand on her head and his other over her shoulder. He looked deep into her eyes and said, "You are a child of God, you are safe and sound, now and forever." He repeated his words three times and added, "You are me, and I am you, because you are a child of the Almighty." The woman's cry stopped at once, and peace began to spread over her once tormented face. Like magic, her expression and posture changed. Even the stress lines on her face disappeared within minutes. She returned to sit in her place in the circle, and another man crawled to Jesus' feet, crying, and asking to heal his son's illness. Jesus continued to heal and talk to several more women and men who asked for his help, until finally there was silence. I heard the cries echo for a moment and then disappear in the depths of the silence that enveloped the circle and sowed in us a sweet all-pervading love. I felt infinite healing through soul-nourishing love. I experienced perfection and all-embracing love, for myself, those around me and to the entire world, wrapped in grace. We sat in a circle yearning and insatiably wanting to absorb more of that love. The sweet scent of oleander was carried in the balmy air, as I felt droplets of sweat running down my back. Like a love addict, I wanted to gulp each word that came out of my teacher's mouth. His simple teachings aimed to take us back to our origin and to keep serving it to us as part of creation's sea of love.

Creation is made of the fabric of unity that is within us, the Godhead. Miriam and I waited a little while for the people to disperse, so that we could talk to Jesus privately about the things that occupied our minds, and he already knew that our teacher Asa had sent us to him.

Finally, after a long wait, he beckoned us with his loving gaze to approach. We came closer and sat with him in the shade of the trees. Mary Magdalene, his partner and senior pupil, who was sitting next to him, got up and left. Mary was a beautiful woman with long red hair and serene dark eyes. She returned minutes later with a large pitcher of water and clay cups, which she placed at Jesus' feet. He poured fresh, clear water into the cups and handed them to us. We rushed to gulp down the water with great thirst as we did his words that flowed after he gave us a good look. Jesus could see into us and far beyond into distant, unseen realms. He looked at my beloved Miriam, who sat quietly next to me, holding my hand for support. Jesus turned to us and said, "Mental suffering also has another, hidden meaning. Every human soul that comes into the world reveals itself and can learn to unite the element of humanity with the spiritual divinity within it. You too, Asaf, are walking your path and developing the ability to concentrate on the inner dimension.

"The light you form inside you radiates and attracts certain people to enter your life sphere, to experience a healing light. This is natural, and you should not have to fight for it. Spiritual work is first of all existence, and only then action. When the spiritual light within is balanced, the healing you give to others flows easily without any excessive physical or mental effort. Different people will come into your life seeking therapy. Now is the right time for you to move to the center of your inner soul in silence. You and Miriam have to come to terms with what you have gone through with acceptance that your cousin Nimrod's learning cycle contributes and complements personal growth. It would be enough for you to be there for his soul, even if he has already returned to his maker. Crisis leads to a deep inner transformation through the cosmic order of creation.

"If a part of you does not want change, or if something hinders transformation, this leads to a crisis. The obstacle within you does not allow growth and a renewed inner adjustment to your soul, in harmony with creation. Allowing the crisis to occur without blocking it is a situation in which you experience pain, difficulties, uncertainty, and insecurity, followed by a new path in place of the old.

"An external factor can never heal the trauma and injury you have experienced. Only you can do this through wisdom and applying the strength that exists within you. I ask you to trust in creation and return to your inner light, the very one that connects you directly to God. The light that provides love and confidence in you now shines from the heart and asks to channel your attention on him. To receive the help of the Creator, you must know how to ignite the light within yourself and believe in it.

"If you remain too long in sorrow and sadness, you will eventually lose the connection between your soul and the source. The time for your transformation has come, my dear brothers and sisters. I ask you even in these grim times to continue to focus on your destiny. Do it with your head held high in a reality of love and harmony. You must know that everything you ask for and that is needed for your complete fulfillment, awaits, and will be provided.

"You must walk this earth without fear of the darkness, because light is stronger. The light will never be defeated. It waits with love and patience until you reach out and open the door of your heart. What prevents you from achieving inner peace and clarity is fear. It appears due to the lack of trust, inspiration, and wisdom. When you leave your heart out of your life, and move away from the center of your being, you move away from serenity and inner peace. Every time you practice breathing and contact the core of your soul, you will return to a renewed clarity within yourself, fearlessly experiencing difficult emotions without sinking or holding on to them. You can look fear in the eye and send ascension energy directly to it.

"You are your own Messiah. Only you can open the door of your heart and receive light from it. This requires courage, strength, and trust in yourself and your calling out of your own ability to transform a difficult emotion and return to rest in the center of your heart. Believe in the quiet, peaceful, clear voice within you. God and I walk beside you, loving and wanting you to receive the love. Allow me to serve you on your path to light."

When he finished his wonderful speech, we all continued to sit together in silence, wrapped in our love, until Mary Magdalene invited Miriam to join the group of women in their community, whom she guided and taught as a senior spiritual teacher alongside Jesus. Miriam said goodbye to me and followed her, leaving me sitting with Jesus for a few hours in silence, in deep introspection, until the sun went down.

Miriam

Chapter 1

I followed Mary Magdalene to the village of Magdala by the Sea of Galilee. Asaf will join me in a few days, and from there we will continue to his parents' house in the village at the foot of Mount Tabor. A group of us women walked with Mary Magdalene an entire day until we finally arrived at Magdala, a village located close to the blue lake, where the local residents make a living from fishing and date picking. We spent the night hosted by the women of the community and started off the following day with a refreshing dip in the Sea of Galilee and a shared breakfast... Mary later came to pick me up from the courtyard of a house surrounded by an arbor of date branches, giving shade that served as a meeting place for women. I joined the ten young women who were sitting under the shade engaged in the craft of making baskets of all kinds – open baskets, lidded baskets, with and without handles all from date leaves. Some leaves interwoven, others made of strips and fresh stems cut to shape and size. There were stacks of large baskets designed for storage and transportation, and smaller baskets for storage of foods such as cookies or fish. There were also wide deep or flat baskets designed for selling fruits and vegetables. The women also made baby carriers, fans to expel flies, hats, and mats in different shapes, elongated and round. We sat down on low stools, on a seat made of ropes woven from leaves, and on a clean clay floor, which they swept with a broom made of date threads.

The women greeted Mary and me with joy and hugs, as they put their craft work aside for a later time and gathered in a circle, sitting on the small wooden stools in the center of the shaded area. Mary and I sat down, and she began to speak, "Blessed are you, women of Magdala," and then introduced me as a healer through dance and song from the Essene Unity Congregation who has come to join and learn the work of light, and later teach in the village by Mount Tabor. The women of the group welcomed me, and I felt like I was being taken into a warm home.

Mary continued to speak and impart her wisdom. "My beloved Jesus spoke to me recently about things that I will share with you regarding the understanding of man and woman and the relationship between them. Feminine light and masculine light are ancient lights, around which much happens and will happen in the future process of development on earth. These are two faces of the one God, hence they are not opposite or separated lights, but rather two sides of one being. The male light is focused outward. It is the part that drives external manifestation that causes spirit to take form. It has a strong creative power, and it allows us to separate ourselves from the one source, to be unique. The female light is the light of the primordial source, the light of the home, the flowing light, the pure being, a light that has not yet been realized inside. The feminine essence is broad, all-embracing and does not differentiate or set us apart from the source. The female light and the male light are united, joyfully merged with each other in creation.

"In an ancient time in creation, before humanity was created, a battle took place between the lights, and they have since been perceived as opposites. However, in the male light there is a core of the female and vice versa, even though the basic unity was forgotten and disappeared, and the lights became opposites. In the past there were times when the female light had a power and advantage in human culture, and it would propel the male light and ruled it incorrectly. When that time passed and changed, the male light prevailed. The male light today has started to misuse its power, in such a way that the female light is weakened and has yet to fulfil its purpose and being. The female light and the male light are inter-reliant, and when they clash it results in destruction. But in this process, there are changes and there will be more changes in the further development of the human race. The feminine light awakens, and its star shines as human development increases, and the masculine light will change and be redefined. This will happen when there is a reunification with a male light or a mature and balanced male light, thus allowing the feminine light to flourish and succeed once again.

"The male light, in its current and old role as a violent, malevolent aggressor that acts in ways of anger and devastation, will transform and cease to lead the world. However, this also depends on the way in which we, humans, relate to aggression and cruelty. If we continue to react in ways of anger and resentment, we will be sucked into obliteration, strife, and the inner evil within ourselves. When these feelings arise in us, it is important that we know how to stop and return to peace within ourselves.

"We must revisit the wisdom of the heart and gift of oversight without letting feelings of helplessness overcome us and we victimize ourselves to ruin. Aggression and evil will not be able to harm one who does not allow them to penetrate their sphere of light. When you learn to respond without hatred or anger, you do not attract them into your life's light sphere.

"Heal the male vibration and find the balance and the light, to protect the female vibration well. Do this knowing how to take care of yourselves, my sisters, as it is from there that you will express your uniqueness and live knowing complete fulfillment. Shine into your surroundings without fear. Cooperation between these two lights is of immense importance. The rebirth of the male vibration will first be realized in each of the sexes separately. All of you, my sisters, shield the ancient sphere of light within you. It is your birthright to make the partnership between the male light and the female light equal and full of joy and love."

Mary finished speaking and let the village women go on their ways before engaging with me in a private conversation. "Miriam, let us meet tomorrow morning to talk by the Sea of Galilee," she said. "I would like to prepare you for the full moon ceremony, which will take place in the moon hutch a day from now when the full moon appears. You are a female leader, and I want to empower you and confirm you into your feminine power, even before you become a mother and have children."

I excitedly agreed to meet with her and went on my way to help my hosts with their housework.

Chapter 2

At dawn, Mary picked me up from the house where I was staying and took me to the Sea of Galilee by the village. The light began to illuminate the sky as we sat down together near the water, by a small circle of stones, inside which remained the residue of burnt branches from last night's bonfire. She lit a small fire against the morning chill, and then took out a small loaf of bread from a cloth sash she was carrying, as breakfast. The morning, before sunrise, was magical, and in addition to the sound of waves gently moving and caressing the shore, birds were chirping. She divided the bread between us, and we ate it together, getting to know each other through conversation. It became clear quickly that we would go on together for the rest of our lives as family. I asked her where she was born and raised, and she told me briefly about the village of Magdala, and how she later met Jesus, who helped her heal her soul. After that, she became his pupil and partner. She was a few years older than me and radiated self-confidence. I felt that we were sisters with a common calling and destiny. I looked at her soft and beautiful face and her red hair that flowed gracefully over her shoulders. I was thirsty for her wise words.

"Today I will guide you in preparation for the blood rite, and in the exercise of feminine power during a night of a full moon, which will be conducted in a special place where the women of the village gather to celebrate the moon. This rite pertains to sacred sexuality and will occur at night. You are a leader who is destined to work with the women of the community you will live with, with Asaf as your partner.

"The knowledge that I will share with your today will be passed down by you to the women of your community and to your future daughters."

"Thank you," I replied. "I am full of gratitude to you and for your guidance as there are so many questions that I would like to ask you."

"I will be happy to answer them and guide you as a mother and sister," she said and continued, "I will begin with the sacred sexuality and its connection with sacred dance, which is also your destiny and mission. Sex is a dance of the sphere of light and contact with the life force of creation. A kind of proclamation of human beings about their being in the physical reality. When a relationship between a man and a woman is based on proper values, it brings trust, sharing, and closeness in sexuality. It also brings passion, pleasure, love, and self-worth.

"The sexual sphere of light is emotional, and when sexuality exists between a man and a woman, both receive their partners' sphere of light and the essence of their life patterns. The sexual sphere of light is sacred and evokes vibration, love, and joy. The merging of the light spheres creates a third sphere between them. Sexuality also floods you with unresolved and hidden feelings, and a deep connection that can restore the entirety of being, revive it and heal the body, soul and spirit. The experience of orgasm connects to the spirit and rearranges the cells, infusing them with renewal. The sensation in the genitals and the entire body is a gateway to all centers of light throughout the universe. The sexual act of love leads to deep breathing, which increases the power of the blood, and it awakens a clear and heightened awareness. Blood increases life span and as well as our resilience and overall health. When we make love, we awaken the energy that is at the base of creation and at the base of the spine, welcoming the light into our lives. The snake-like light comes to teach you the dance of life. This energy can rise and climb along your back and spiral out. When we slow down the rhythm of the sexual dance, we can collect energy that can be sent out as love that awakens our surroundings toward harmony and peace. Women tend to pay attention to various aspects of life and create a deeper connection with their bodies. They are naturally connected to the power found in the blood and the power of the lunar cycles that activates the blood in the menstrual cycle. Pregnancy and childbirth can also strengthen a woman's connection with her own body.

"When women accept their bodily functions and their menstrual cycle, they become stronger. When the woman receives her menstrual blood, the gates of the spirit are opened to her, and she can ascend to many aspects of life in the universe. The female blood must gain recognition and respect, and like the man's white semen, which is also a potion of life, so is the blood in a woman. Partnership and relationship, in which the life forces of the white sperm and the red blood manifest are crucial.

"When a woman gets older and stops menstruating, she still lives in power. As the woman matures, she treasures her blood and preserves its power. At a later stage of life, a woman receives a powerful gift of wisdom that enables her to control her body and spirit.

"A well-balanced woman knows that she is the source of herself, and in partnership with a man she becomes a greater source of emanation. A woman does not necessarily need a partner, but it is a natural process, to build strength together as part of human development that is in harmony with the body and spirit of the human being. The woman and the man are supposed to develop individually, while gaining the inner balance between the female and male parts of the sphere of light. This light and power are likened to a snake, which can become a path of light that fills the entire being. I invite you, Miriam, my sister, to immerse yourself in the mikvah in the water of the Sea of Galilee in preparation for the ceremony that will take place tonight at the moon hutch. It will be a full moon tonight, and many of the women of the village share their bodies' monthly cycle together. This will be an opportunity to meet the strength of your power in the company of the women of Capernaum."

I went to dip in the water of the lake mikvah with Miriam. We dipped three times, and the water covered our heads. When we came out of the water all refreshed, we parted ways. I waited for the time of night when the women of the village would meet in the moon hutch to which I will go with my host in Capernaum.

Chapter 3

The full moon hangs in the sky as its silver light illuminates the path I walk with my host Rebecca, talking about what will happen tonight in the moon hutch. Knowing that I have never experienced a gathering at the moon hutch as the rest do each month, Rebecca explains that it is a cycle experienced as life and death inside the bodies of women. Women bleed and die during the full moon and then are reborn with the new moon. The cycle of fertile women is in sync with mother earth. Most women in the village experience the bloody period together. They retire from the rest of the community to the specific area where the men do not approach, for a sacred, quality time together. A woman in her bloody period is considered at the height of her power and has the ability to give and receive visions to her sisters and daughters. It is a time of dreams with significance to the entire community. At this time, they are exempt from all the usual tasks. They rest and spend time together, telling stories about themselves. They consult with each other, learn about the secrets of cooking, about men, about sex and other diverse topics. As only women have done and will continue to do, we share, thus allowing young women to learn from their elders while wisdom and important knowledge is passed on from an early age.

"The full moon is a time when a girl becomes a woman and parts with everything she will never be able to allow herself again. She receives four blessings from four women, who symbolize the four elements in a grand celebration of abundance." Rebecca finished her explanation, when we found ourselves near a large round hutch, wrapped in white cloth, topped with a thatch of palm branches, perforated thus allowing the women sitting under it to see the night stars and the full moon. We entered naked into the hutch, which was lit by candlelight and the light of the full moon, and we breathed in the scents of myrrh incense. The atmosphere was happy and about ten young women, and I among them, received a foot massage with frankincense oil from the older women. I lay down on soft pillows, and I felt the massage relaxing my soul and cleansing me of negative thoughts, fears, and mental barriers. Then I was asked to drink a few drops of my own blood mixed and diluted with water. During the ceremony, the women sang and beat drums to the rhythm of a heartbeat as four women surrounded me and blessed me for the unity of the four elements in my life. Fire, earth, air, and water coalesced in me, the oil on my feet warmed me and stimulated my senses, and the scents of white lilies filled my being.

The other young women who were lying around me on mattresses in the moon hutch were in a trance-dream state, like me, and each received blessings from the four women. They began to speak the special words of the moon while taking deep breaths and expanding their hearts. They received messages and prayed to the white entity, who gave them visions and messages about peace and harmony within and around them. Mary approached and sat to my left, placing her warm hand on my heart. I felt an accelerated heartbeat and saw a ball of warm orange light penetrating my body and spreading to every part of it. Magdalene instructed me to take deep breaths to receive a vision of power which would shed light on my current path. She placed her hand in the center of my forehead and transferred yet another ball of orange light. My soul began to travel quickly to a luminous place surrounded by green trees, and a bright, hazy female figure surrounded by golden light began walking in front of me. The figure and I walked in each other's direction until we were face to face. To my amazement, the figure standing in front of me was the older me, decades into the future. She smiled warmly and looked at me with love, oozing confidence and strength. Behind her, I saw that there was another young figure who was about my age now, who resembled me and Assaf. The young girl was noble, with deep blue eyes and long golden hair. She told me her name was Sarah and gave me a gold staff topped with a blue sapphire. She referred to me as 'Miriam my sorceress mother' and thanked me for training her for her vocation. The blue sapphire suddenly detached from the golden wand and flew around in the air, then penetrated the center of my forehead. The present, past, and future mingled and united, and I knew that all the knowledge I needed was given to me by the future, and that when my daughter is born, I will train her for her mission in spreading love and healing in the world.

After this vision, I fell into a deep and long sleep, in which I was unconscious and dreamless. When I woke up, I learned from the women who were with me in the moon hutch that I had been in this dream vision state for three whole days.

Asaf

Chapter 1

This morning, I went with Jesus and his disciples to Capernaum, to visit the community of pupils and gather his apostles for the work of light on planet Earth. My beloved Miriam has been there for a few weeks in the company of Mary Magdalene and the community of women she leads. With much longing, I look forward to seeing Miriam and to sharing with her experiences and feelings that we each went through separately this past month. As we entered Capernaum, I saw Miriam running toward me, and we hugged and kissed at length.

"It is so wonderful to see you again, Asaf. I learned many things from Mary and the women of Capernaum," Miriam said with much excitement.

We saw that Jesus began to walk with Mary toward the Sea of Galilee, and we joined them. When the villagers noticed him, they came out and followed. A large crowd of believers and disciples joined and sat on the shore of the lake to listen to his words. Miriam and I sat among them in the first row so as to be close to our teacher and listen thirstily to him speak.

"Brothers and sisters, you are the keepers of the Gate of Light," Jesus, son of Joseph, began to tell his flock. "Just wait a little longer, because the old world will gradually disappear, and with it, old power structures based on a thirst for power. They will lose their strength and melt into nothingness at the bottom of the sea." Jesus turned his gaze to the waters of the Sea of Galilee and gazed dreamily into the distant horizon. "All of you, my brothers and sisters, are part of this essential transformation. In your transition from the old to the new, your being will radiate a new light. Your sphere of light and your surroundings will change shape, affect your environment and all the things you will pull into your life. The state of your being will then change the state of your life experience.

"When many people become a group, and many groups follow, they will cultivate spheres of light, transform them and draw the kingdom of heaven to the face of the earth. It will be a total change that will begin with you as individuals, my brothers and sisters. You, my messengers, will become the 'gatekeepers,' who open the new gate of light on the face of planet Earth. Since this gate is now closed, the light cannot enter and seep into the soil. It is important that you awaken your spirits, my beloved messengers, so that you know and feel what you came to do and the purpose of your soul. You are all working and learning to realize the changes within you primarily. You were born to learn to do inner work, work that lifts the spheres of light out of love and harmony. This is how you will transform all of reality into beauty and truth. My spiritual messengers, know that it does not matter what you do in your life, whether you are fishermen, farmers, healers, merchants, or teachers. Your mood and your being are agents of transformation, and the light you radiate changes the sphere you are in, because the source of the change is your essence.

"Feel now the light spheres here on the shore of the Sea of Galilee, raise and accept it into your heart, because once you do, your light can flow, enter, and leave you, here throughout the land of Israel. Remember that every time you open your heart to creation, God shines, bringing light and radiance to you. You are the people who open the gate, and God thanks you and wraps you with his love. The earth is beginning to change now, and a new world will rise from the ashes of the old world, as change begins in your heart and your emotions. All human beings have emotions that throw them out of balance, but you can refine them. Accept the responsibility, knowing the source of the light within you.

"Brothers and sisters, who are gathered in Capernaum in the Land of Israel, find out what is blocking your heart and change it. This will give you calm and balance, peace and quiet to fill your heart. This light is within your reach and only you can open the gate from the heart and accept the kingdom of heaven in your heart and in your soul. I ask you here and now, my brothers and sisters, feel the sphere of my light in your heart. Feel the inner space that lets go of the old, making room for a fresh light, so that all the old fears, sorrow, and anger that you have incurred in life, shall integrate into the light within you. Know that you are strong, and that you will succeed in doing this. Look every day into the depths of your being and find the light burning there. Release anger from your heart, and introduce into your core the acceptance of things as they are. Release the sadness and pain without dwelling on them too much. Trust in the great light in you and in the Creator, believe that everything you need will be given to you. The light is stronger. The light will never be defeated. It is waiting with love and patience for the moment you open the door to your heart. Let go of all fear and worry, as you are your own Messiah. There are no other Messiahs except you. Only you can open the gate to your heart. Only you pull a positive reality and help yourselves and the earth. You, the brave and the bold, believe in yourselves and what you came to accomplish in your life, return to the anchor that is in your heart. Stop getting stuck in drama and fear, because chaos is not true; only peaceful silence is the truth. Return once again to your heart, which knows that you are never alone. Always remember that the Creator walks by your side and with you, as you walk the path of the transformation of the heart."

Chapter 2

A year has passed since Miriam and I returned to the village at the foot of Mount Tabor. The year of mourning for Nimrod's death passed, and when we informed the family that we were getting married, the joy was mixed with sadness. Asa my teacher left the Essenes and returned to Jerusalem, as he told me he would, when Miriam and I also left Unity Congregation. He was invited to our wedding and sent me a letter by courier. He wrote that he would come accompanied by one woman named Ruth, whom he almost married when he was young. He explained that Ruth married another man and was since widowed, yet she always remembered him with great love. Ruth, as I understand it, accepted his quick marriage proposal when he asked for her hand in marriage a month ago, and since then they have been living together with all of Ruth's children and grandchildren.

On the day of our wedding, many of the villagers and all of our family members gathered in the orchard of fruit and olive trees by Nimrod's parents' house. Miriam and I wanted to honor them by holding the ceremony at their home, as well as to console them over the fact that Nimrod would never marry. Nimrod's family members were moved by the gesture and his mother prepared Miriam as the bride. She treated her like a daughter and the woman she was grooming to marry Nimrod's brother and found great comfort in that role.

I stood surrounded by men. Nimrod's brother and father did not leave me alone for a single moment. They laughed and joked with me about what was expected of me as a future father and husband and about the gravity of the challenge. They teased me and were genuinely nice to me in their own way. If only they had been a little softer towards Nimrod, I thought sadly, perhaps his fate would now be different and his life less complicated. The wedding in the orchard of fruit and olive trees was held in a small grape arbor, decorated with lilies and a white fabric spread out as a special and beautiful canopy. The women of the village and my mother among them accompanied Miriam to the canopy with song, tambourine, and flute melodies. Nimrod's mother and older sister held her arms as companions and led her to the canopy. From the other direction, from my house in the village, my father and Nimrod's father walked next to me, holding my arms, and behind us an entourage of the village men, chanting joyous holiday prayers at the top of their lungs.

The village rabbi was waiting under the canopy, dressed in traditional clothes, with a white tallit draped over his head and shoulders. We, the bride and groom, were set in the center of the arbor, close to one another. Miriam wore a white dress with a gold hem, and her golden hair was combed into many braids, and her head was adorned with a wreath of white roses. Her deep blue eyes looked at me with great love, and I felt extremely fortunate to marry my beautiful beloved

Miriam. The rabbi began to say his blessings and chanted "the sound of mirth and gladness, the voice of bridegroom and bride,"

I was so overcome with joy that for a moment, I forgot Nimrod was not alive. I felt that we were completing a circle of healing and standing at the threshold of a new gate on the path of love, and that together with my beloved Miriam, I would know freedom and align with what I wanted more than anything - heaven on earth. When the wedding ceremony was over, I saw Asa standing in the company of an older woman, about his age, a short and delicate woman, with her black hair tossed aside. They stood embraced and united under the trees, and they seemed to love and respect each other very much. Asa and his new wife Ruth looked at me and Miriam and sent us joy filled smiles.

Asa approached, hugged, and congratulated me before saying, "When I left the Essenes about a week after you, I realized that shortly after that, the Ark of the Covenant disappeared from the hidden cave in Qumran. Old Judah sent a messenger to search for me in Jerusalem, so that I could explain to him why the Ark of the Covenant disappeared so soon after I had left. I answered him in the scroll that I sent by the messenger, that the mystery is great, and that I believe that the Ark was transferred to other keepers to be discovered in the future, generations ahead from now."

"I have a feeling Asaf," said Asa, "that I will come back to train you as my successor and teach you many secrets. I will also come back to train your daughter, whom you will call Sarah, and together we will continue to charge the field of light of planet Earth. I will return to teach you, my son, and later share our work with little Sarah when she grows up. Sarah, your eldest daughter, will one day become a trailblazing female leader from a long line of female leaders descended from the line of David.

What a wonderful way this would be to continue Nimrod's path, who will continue to ascend with us in spirit. Miriam was indeed at the beginning of her pregnancy when we got married, but I stopped being surprised by the prophetic vision of my magical teacher Asa. I just gently placed my hand on my wife Miriam's pregnant belly, over the white wedding dress she was wearing, and I felt the fetus 'Sarah' kicking lightly inside her. Our daughter's soul sang to me in the language of light that is beyond words,

"Asaf, to the place we go and from which we run,
We will rise up and ascend to the One."

-The End-

Printed in Great Britain
by Amazon